Book 2,

Surrendering Stinkin' Thinkin'

Series

You're Amazing

Hannah Arduini

Julie Arduini

ISBN: 978-1-7336876-0-7

Published by Surrendered Scribe Media, Youngstown, Ohio, 44514

http://juliearduini.com

Surrendering Stinkin' Thinkin'

Book 2

You're Amazing

Hannah Arduini & Julie Arduini

Surrendering Stinkin' Thinkin'

You're Beautiful---Hayley Atkinson withdraws from her friends and new opportunities with the new mentoring group, Linked, after she is told a lie that she believes is true about herself. Sabrina Wayson is a mentor in Linked who feels she can't encourage girls because she's struggling as much as they are. Can they surrender the lies and find freedom?

You're Amazing--- Jazmin West is in the eighth grade and is a natural at dance, until she comes across changes that leave her feeling unworthy. Her mentor, Lena Calloway, is a mom of young children and she mourns the carefree days she had. When Lena and her husband attend an event and she's asked what does she do, her answer sends her on a journey to find out how valuable her life really is.

Can Lena and Jazmin surrender the lies they believe and find freedom in the truth that they are amazing?

Coming Soon:

You're Brilliant---Bethany has a lot of changes in her life as a new teenager, but she decides to tackle it with her offbeat humor. No one laughs with her, and even worse, her classmates abandon her, making Bethany feel rejected. Mrs. Cheri is a pastor's wife who loves her life, but new commitments have her overwhelmed. A joke aimed at her goes straight to her heart, and she's convinced she's not good at anything she's been asked to do. Can these two stop believing lies about themselves and embrace the changes in their life with laughter and grace.

A Message for Readers:

This series was inspired by Hannah after a tough transition to junior high. Instead of giving up and becoming bitter, Hannah decided to take the lessons she learned and create a series for girls her age. Julie (Hannah's mom,) has a passion for mentoring. As she listened to Hannah create characters, Julie realized there was a message in Hannah's work for women, too.

Each book in the Surrendering Stinkin' Thinkin' Series uses the theme of letting go of a lie the characters believed. There will be two key characters in each book. One, a junior high student, and the other, a woman out of school. It's our desire to see girls of all ages (even grandmas!) read these books and find freedom and hope in them.

Hannah created the storyline, character names and traits, plot points, and conflict. She had the vision for the cover, and directed Julie in the design. Julie wrote out Hannah's vision and managed the writing and publishing process, staying true to Hannah's creation. *You're Amazing* is a work of fiction, but a message of hope for you.

Dedication

To females of all ages who have
been told or who have ever felt they
weren't good enough:

You are amazing!

CHAPTER ONE

Jazmin West

The last of the firetrucks pulls away, and the smell of destroyed dreams fills my lungs. Mom's hand on my back is the first sensation I've had since Miss Elena called with the news.

The dance studio is gone.

Mom reaches for my shoulders and turns me so we're face to face. "Jazmin, this isn't the end of your dancing life. This is a terrible setback—nothing more."

My lip quivers, so I clamp down with my teeth in hopes I can control something, anything. Like my ocean of tears ready to fall.

Miss Elena, Dance Academy founder and my teacher, approaches us. Her usually tight bun is loose, and wavy strands of black hair frame her face. Her brown eyes seem dulled, and not by the smoke. "Sweet Jazmin, it was so kind of you to come and make sure I was okay. There's nothing we can do here. You should go home."

"Do the firefighters know what happened?" Mom leaves my side to give my teacher a hug. Miss Elena pauses as a sob escapes and she covers her mouth with her hand for a moment.

Her words are slow to come, probably marked by exhaustion. "Nothing definitive, but the chief mentioned possible faulty wiring."

I kick at a pebble on the sidewalk before looking to Miss Elena. "What happens now?"

She stretches her hand toward me, cupping my cheek. "We rebuild."

Three Months Later

Bethany Tuttle jumps in front of me, displaying an exaggerated jazz hands move. "Will you gesture like this at the end of your dance today?" She shuffles beside me and together we walk down Center Street Middle School's eighth-grade halls.

I roll my eyes. "As if. I don't know how this new studio will be, but Miss Elena would never allow such a thing."

Bethany stops in front of Miss Wayson's class. "What a shame. Doesn't sound like fun at all. If Hayley and I don't see you, have fun at the new dance place. Don't forget we have Linked tomorrow." She disappears into class and I can hear the teacher, Sabrina Wayson, who is also one of our mentors at our church mentoring ministry.

I sigh, trekking forward to math class two doors down. "Linked. Right. I almost forgot." *Because my focus has been on not freaking out about the different dance location. New teacher. Miss Elena still working on plans to rebuild and encouraging me to move forward instead of waiting.*

Mr. Wexell greets me as soon as I enter the room. "Good morning, Jazmin. Do you mind changing the calendar to September? I forgot to do it with the long weekend."

I nod, flipping the page over. *I hate change*

CHAPTER TWO

Lena Calloway

The yellow blur stops me in my tracks. Without my contacts it's usually hard to focus on the distance, but my stomach drops as I realize what today is. The bus stops at the corner and several elementary-age kids from our street climb on for the first day of school.

A shout from the kitchen table reminds me why my nerves are as frayed as an old sweater. "Mommy! You said you were getting my cereal."

I sigh and return to the task, picking up scattered toys as I navigate my way to the pantry. "Be right there, Alex."

One more year until I can at least have one child in school. Three years until both boys are waiting for that beautiful yellow bus to transport them to school. *Oh, Lord, forgive me. I love being a mom. But, I'm tired.*

Bryce descends the stairs two steps at a time, whistling as he tightens his tie. He smiles as we lock eyes and reaches for the fridge door as I grab the cereal. "I got the milk."

Alex pushes his chubby finger against the tablet screen and scrolls the next video, looking up for a moment. "Daddy's faster than mommy."

Seems like everything's a race when you're five. Maybe twenty-five, too.

Bryce places the milk on the table and messes Alex's hair while I open the oat and nut breakfast and pour it into the bowl. Once I finish, I reach for the milk and find my husband's hand taking mine. "Got anything fun planned today?"

My laugh's as shaky as my milk pouring. "Same old, same old. It's library day."

Bryce squeezes my hand and nods. "Hey, you love the library. On our first date you said one day your book would be on their shelves."

"That was seven years and two kids ago."

My high school love grabs a granola bar from the pantry. "Speaking of two kids, where's Marshall?"

Alex pipes up before panic has time to attack. "Potty."

My sweats and slippers are no match for Bryce's khaki's and loafers. He swings the bathroom door wide open so I have the same view of Marshall's activities that he does.

Bryce checks his watch and sighs. "I'm sorry, I have to go."

"It's okay. I've got it." It's more of a pep talk to myself than a reply.

He messes with Marshall's unruly blond curls, gives me a quick kiss on the top of the head, and leaves me with a three-year-old and a toilet housing about a dozen of Marshall's little racecars.

Marshall holds up a small green tractor. "He lost the race."

I suck in a deep breath and lift the plastic bucket by the tub that's meant for tub toys. "You know cars don't go in the potty, right?"

He glances up at me with those saucer-shaped eyes. "Sorry."

"No more of this, okay? Stay here while I get the cars out and wash us up before breakfast."

"Sorry, Mama."

Fishing in the toilet keeps my emotions in check as I avoid his sweet stare. "I forgive you."

I set the filled bucket aside to sterilize later and start the water for extreme hand washing. Alex shouts something, probably still in the kitchen, but I can't discern what he's saying. "Just a minute, Bud."

Once Marshall and I have cucumber-melon-scented hands, I walk down the hall. "What did you say, Alex?" I pick up my pace as I hear him crying.

"I wanted more cereal but you were busy."

I'm facing his big round eyes and his finger pointing to the table, flooded with milk. Including the tablet, no longer playing music. "Oh, no. No, no, no." I race over and pick up the device, praying it still works. The screen's dead.

Just like my motivation.

You're Amazing

CHAPTER THREE

JAZMIN

The Poise Dance Academy better not be as intimidating as the building looks. I flopped my hands over my hips. Once a school, the brick and ivy structure towers over the homes in the otherwise residential area two miles outside of Youngstown. The windows still showcase faded room numbers. Bass undertones from an inside class surround the property, probably thanks to the old structure and terrible acoustics. *Okay, girl. Time to check this new place out.*

I push on the heavy wooden doors and find the lobby lined with benches filled with adults. Their heads turn toward me as I enter and I offer a meager smile. Most likely parents waiting for their child to finish, they return to their business without giving any response to my greeting.

Miss Elena told me my new class, taught by one of her friends, Miss Valerie, would be in room 103. I pass the cafeteria and locate the room, no longer full of desks and chairs, but with plenty of space. A wooden barre is installed against the wall, and a horizontal mirror above the bar goes across most of the wall area. A woman and a girl about my age are in the corner, playing with a Bluetooth speaker.

I stroll over and clear my throat. "Hi. Is this Intermediate Ballet? Miss Elena told me to come here and ask for Miss Valerie?"

The two straighten and face me, but only the woman smiles. Both are tall, slender, with similar forest green eyes. The girl reminds me of winter, her complexion pale, her blonde hair so light it almost appears white. Also, her gaze toward me is cold. *What's her issue?*

You're Amazing

"Jazmin? I'm Valerie Frost. Elena told me all about you, welcome." She extends her hand and gives a firm handshake before focusing on the other girl. "This is Brittni, my daughter."

Brittni doesn't offer a welcome or a smile. She keeps a stiff stance as she gives her attention to her dusty rose fingernails. "I was the lead in last year's Nutcracker. You probably saw it on TV."

This is where I hear my grandma's loving voice in my head. *Don't sass back, you be the light of Christ, Jazmin West.* Still, the temptation. "I'm sorry, I missed it. I traveled with Miss Elena to DC to attend a senate ball celebrating youth with potential."

Brittni's scowl affects her head to toe. Her eyes narrow, even her bun seems to tighten and freezes her face. Her mom's the opposite. Miss Valerie offers a wide smile.

I focus on my new teacher. "I'm sorry, what was your last name again?"

Brittni spits a reply before her mom can answer. "Frost."

One more look at those chilly green eyes. *Of course it is.*

Before we can engage in a stare down, the door creaks open and another girl who looks to be about my age sashays in with a toothy smile and dark curls that bounce with each step. She carries a faded nylon gym bag that looks older than either of us. Her tennis shoes squeak when she abruptly stops in front of us, the bag landing next to her feet.

Miss Valerie stretches out her hand. "Hi, Valerie Frost. Are you here for intermediate ballet?"

20

The newcomer keeps the grin and shakes her hand. "I'm Emily Santos. I took beginner class in Akron, but that was last winter. I moved here over the summer." She shifts her attention to me. "Hey. I think I saw you at school. Center Street?" She reaches in the bag, pulls out a scrunchie, and piles her hair into a knot on top of her head.

I nod. "I'm Jazmin West. The dance studio I used to go to burned down."

Emily gasps, her chocolate-colored eyes wide. "That's terrible. So, this is your first time here?"

Brittni lets out an exaggerated sigh that could win an Oscar. "My mother isn't paid to listen to chit-chat. Shouldn't you get dressed for class?"

Emily raises an eyebrow and faces Brittni. "I am dressed to dance."

I bite my lip to stop any laughter from squeaking out.

The blonde rolls her eyes and ignores us, moving closer to her mother. "Did you want me to test their skills before the others arrive?"

"How about you check in the other girls as they come in, and I'll work with Emily and Jazmin?" Miss Valerie hands the clipboard to her daughter, who looks like she swallowed a lemon.

Ninety minutes later, Emily and I not only demonstrate our skills but complete our first session of Ms. Valerie's intermediate class. As the other girls disperse and find their parents, Emily grabs her nylon bag and swings it

21

over her shoulders as she heads to the doors. "I think intermediate has different meanings to each teacher. Half that stuff we just did I never heard of in Akron."

I offer a flat smile. "I'm sure it's a broad term. I know Ms. Elena was a stickler on posture. I didn't hear Ms. Valerie point that out at all." *Even though I saw issues with every dancer but Brittni.*

Emily trudges out like she's leaving football practice, not the Poise Academy. She raises her hand to her head and removes some hair pins and pulls on her scrunchie, wild curls falling and framing her face. Instead of putting the hair accessory in her bag or a purse, she pushes it on her wrist like a bracelet.

Ms. Elena would faint to witness this. "I could work with you on turnout and placement if you think it would help."

Her doe-eyes widen, and she slugs my arm hard enough it stings. "Really? Cuz I was ready to quit back there, but I'm on scholarship. My mom would have a fit if I gave up."

I rub my upper arm. "I'll teach you on one condition."

Emily stops and faces me. "Name it."

"Don't hit me. That really hurt!"

She stays silent for a moment, staring at my face. Suddenly she breaks into a cackle. "Sorry, I have five brothers. I usually use my hands for defense."

There's more laughter, but it's coming from behind us, and it's a sarcastic sound I've heard way too many times from former mean-girl-classmate Jade Green. *Brittni.*

I fold my hands against my chest. "What's so funny?"

Brittni approaches us, her expression aghast as if she's stepped in dog mess. "That explains it."

Emily steps closer to Brittni. "What?"

"Why you dance like a linebacker wearing cement for shoes. You're surrounded by brothers who probably have as much grace as you do." Brittni puts a pale hand over her mouth either to stop more giggles or to stop herself from saying more.

I shift my attention back to Emily. "Ignore her. I have a plan if you're interested."

Emily's eyes keep darting toward Brittni. "Let's hear it, Jazmin." She starts walking, and I follow.

"There's this group for girls our age called Linked. We meet monthly with women who bring snacks and encourage us. It's fun. You should come. I could work on the dance steps with you before we start."

Her black spirals bounce as she nods. "Sounds great. Let's trade numbers so you can text me."

As I reach for my purse and dig for my phone, I catch a glimpse of Brittni. She's no longer chuckling, or even smiling. And she's very much alone.

You're Amazing

CHAPTER FOUR

LENA

Six o'clock. I take the steps to the youth wing two at a time, knowing full well it isn't going to make any difference now that I'm thirty minutes late. The Linked meeting's tough to get to when there are mouths to feed and tantrums to wait on, but mentoring girls is a ministry I refuse to quit.

High-pitched laughter echoes as I reach the top of the stairs and turn down the hall. Breathless, I stop and stare at our pastor's wife, Cheri Wayson, smeared in garish makeup as blindfolded Jade Green gives the mentor a makeover.

Bethany Tuttle notices my arrival and stands up. "Lena's here, yay! Did you bring the brownies? Yours are the best." Bethany rubs her stomach in circles.

My belly feels like I ate bricks for dinner. Guilt flows through my digestion system like a boat on rough waters. I shake my head. "I'm sorry. I completely forgot."

Sabrina Wayson, our recent college graduate and current middle school teacher, pops up and traipses to the counter. "Hey Jade, you can take your blindfold off now. Nice work with that lipstick on the forehead." She giggles as she lifts foil off a pan. "Lena, no worries. I've got you covered."

Everyone swarms on that brownie dish faster than bees to honey. I stay still, biting my lip in hopes it keeps the tears at bay. *There was a time I was the young girl who was organized and beloved.* Cheri turns and sees I haven't moved. She gestures for me to join them. "You have a lot on your plate, sweetheart. We're just glad you're here. Right, girls?"

A chorus of "mmhmm's" fill the air as they all continue to stuff brownies into their mouths. For the junior high girls, they confess any food at Linked is most likely their version of dinner.

"I promise to make it up to you. How about pumpkin rolls next month?"

Hayley offers a fist bump and a loud "Yes!"

Now to make sure I don't forget. I walk over to Hayley and put my arm around her and squeeze her shoulder. These girls bring me to life. As I glance over toward Jade and see her extra-short shorts, I remember what else they do. Accelerate my prayer life.

Cheri flashes a smile and clears her throat. "Now that we've all had our caffeine and chocolate for the evening, Jazmin, will you introduce your friend?"

Jazmin stands and directs her hands toward the taller girl with long, curly black hair and a toothpaste-model smile. "This is Emily Santos. She used to live in Akron, but now she resides in Youngstown. We're in the same dance class together."

Sabrina dabs the corners of her mouth with a napkin. "That's right, you started at the new place. Emily, was it your first class there, too?"

The girl nods. "Yep. Jazmin is awesome. She breezed through Miss Val's class like it was nothin'. Girl even promised to help me out. Good thing, cuz I need it."

I perk up when she mentions Val. "Valerie Frost?"

Jazmin tilts her head and focuses on me. "Yeah. You know her?"

All eyes are on me. I swallow and shrug. "It's been years. I used to babysit her little girl." I look at the teenagers around the table. "Actually, she's probably your age, now."

Jazmin looks like she choked on a bug. "You babysat Brittni Frost? The ice princess?"

Two hours later, I pull into the garage, noticing the downstairs lights are on. *Please, Bryce, be the only one up.* I park and take a moment to close my eyes and take a deep breath. I have no idea what I'll be facing once I enter the house.

Bryce is in the kitchen pouring juice into a sippy cup. "Hey, how was Linked and youth group?"

My mind is only on the drink. "Why are you pouring juice into Marshall's cup this late? Aren't they in bed?"

Before he can answer, two streaks come running through the kitchen pushing their toy dump trucks at a speed I'd expect to see on a race track. They leave as fast as they enter, but it's clear no one's sleeping and this isn't the first cup of juice of the night. "I kept them up so you could say goodnight."

Every smile and good feeling I had earlier drains from me as reality sets in. These sugared up boys need order and I have to put my mean-mom hat on and get them to bed. "You didn't have to do that, Bryce. And you definitely don't give them juice to drink at night." My sigh could win an Academy award.

Bryce puts the carton on the counter. "Sorry, Babe. I thought I was helping."

I shake my head and drag myself into the living room where chaos reigns. Alex is playing demolition with his truck, banging it repeatedly against his brother's vehicle. "Boys! It is way past your bedtime. You know the rules. Pick up toys so we can wash up."

Alex opens his mouth, probably to protest, but the steely look he sees coming from me renders him silent. Marshall even takes his hands off the toy in a surrender gesture. They both scurry about the room, putting things back in the box before marching to their bathroom.

Bryce slowly enters the living room and wisely says nothing. Still thinking about the juice, I huff out of there and find the boys splashing water on each other. "What's going on?" My bellow's so loud I frighten them with my sudden appearance.

"Sorry, Mama." Alex's voice shakes. Marshall flat out starts to cry.

"Let's finish up. Marshall, let me help you with your teeth." I prepare his toothbrush and try to work it into his mouth, but he has the too-tired sobs happening that turn into hiccups. "Marshall, c'mon. It's late. You need to get to bed."

Bryce pops his head in and surveys the situation. "Maybe he can have one night without brushing his teeth?"

My eyes narrow as I point the little toothbrush in his direction, toothpaste flying off as I shake it with each word. "He's off the rails because you kept them up too late. And gave them juice." I attempt to brush the youngest's teeth again, finally finding success. Bryce disappears, and I move on with the bedtime routine.

Both kids are in their beds, tucked in, stories finished, prayers completed. I give each a kiss and am about to turn off the light when Alex sits up. "Mama?"

"Yes?"

"Why are you always mad?"

You're Amazing

CHAPTER FIVE

JAZMIN

The next morning, before I have to catch the bus, I'm stuffing the last of my cream cheese bagel in my mouth, the text ding sounds on my phone.

Emily. *I think we have the same lunch period together. Wanna hang?*

A dab of cream cheese drops on my screen as I reply. *Absolutely. I eat with Hayley and Beth, you met them last night.*

Awesome. See you then.

I click off the phone and grab my backpack when Grandma enters the kitchen. She meanders over to the counter, probably checking if I cleaned up the toaster area before clearing her throat. "Have you heard anything from dance since last class?"

"You mean from Ms. Valerie? No. Something wrong?" I ease off the backpack and place it by my feet.

She shakes her head but doesn't look me in the eye. "I have a voicemail. She wondered if you could come a little early before the next class."

I shrug. "Did you forget to pay her?"

Now Grandma chooses to focus on me with a narrow gaze. "No. Very funny. I thought maybe something happened. You mentioned her daughter not being very kind. I was nervous you sassed her."

I roll my eyes and pick up the bag. "It was tempting, not gonna lie. But I knew better than to mouth off and face you later. I gotta go. The bus waits for no one."

She bridges the gap between us and gives a quick hug. "Have a great day. Be smart."

The door slams shut before I can answer. *Be smart. I know she doesn't mean that she wants me to only do well in school. Grandma's making sure I keep my attitude in check.*

Once I'm in my regular seat with earbuds in, I think about what else she said. What does Ms. Val want to talk about?

Hayley, Bethany, Emily and I waste no time during lunch discussing what possible scenarios could take place when I meet with Ms. Val.

Beth's always down for social events, so her mind goes to a celebration. "Maybe she wants you in charge of a fundraiser for your old dance place so there can be a fundraiser to help re-build."

Hayley shakes her head and picks up her fork. "No way. Dance studios are places of business. Your current teacher wants you to stay forever, it's money in her pocket. Why would she want to be a part of helping you return to your original stomping ground? Pun intended."

I roll my eyes. You never have to wonder what Hayley's thinking.

Emily sets her milk carton down with enough force that white splatter hits her curls. "You two weren't there. I was. Ms. Val's gonna ask Jazmin to forgive her for having such an ice queen for a daughter. You should meet this Brittni chick. I think her blood is blue."

Beth leans in with a whisper. "For real?"

Her innocence sends the rest of us into a fit of giggles. I'm the first to sober. "I'll know soon enough. Class starts at four, so I'll head there right after school. I'm sure of one thing."

Hayley stabs at the meatloaf brick. "What's that?"

"None of your ideas are going to be my reality."

By the time I jog home to grab my dance bag and sneak a chocolate chip cookie, it's fifteen minutes before class when I greet Ms. Val. Her blond hair is in a classic bun, but it doesn't seem to make her face tight and sour like it does when Brittni wears the same style.

"Oh, good. Your grandmother got my message. I wanted to propose something to you and see what you think."

My mouth opens slightly as Bethany's words come to mind. "You want me to host a fundraiser?"

Ms. Val tilts her head like she's trying to study me. "Um, no. I wondered if you'd like to move up to advanced."

I straighten. "Really? I thought Poise Academy hosts Intermediate and Intermediate 2? I haven't completed that yet."

She smiles. "No, you haven't. We also feature junior and women levels. I'd like you to consider advanced women. The class starts next week. It's no change in fee, so you're all set there."

My stomach flip-flops. *I never expected this.* "But...I'm thirteen."

The doors open and a group of girls enter, chattering. I glance their way, then back at Ms. Val. She places a hand on my shoulder. "There's absolutely no pressure, Jazmin. I've watched you and you have natural talent. You're bored in this class, I can tell. You've mastered the techniques. I'd like to give you a challenge."

I slowly nod and try to swallow. "That would be a big one. What would I be doing different than I am now?"

More laughter erupts behind me. I want to focus on her answer. I also want to know where Brittni is in case she's got a bitter comment to toss my way.

"You would have classes a few times a week, and the expectation is you'd be consistently demonstrating your strong foundational technique but challenged with pushing for higher extensions with correct positioning and the standard for turns increase as well. We're looking for clean executions and that you push yourself. We do quite a bit of barre work, and that's with minimal instruction time. You'll also need to know combinations and counts. We incorporate lengthier pointe work as well, so it's important demi-pointe be mastered. Dance is an art that always has room for improvement. It requires you to give everything you have. You may feel challenged at first, but I believe you would blend into this level with grace and beauty and see your technique improve."

I take a deep breath. "Do you need an answer today?"

She shook her head. "Not at all. Talk to your family. Like I said, Women's Advanced starts next week."

Before I can reply, a high-pitched squeak sends the hairs on the back of my neck straight up. "Mother? Did you just invite Jazmin to Women's Advanced?"

I turn to find sharp daggers targeted my way, courtesy of Brittni's cold stare. A few steps behind her is Emily, who stops so fast she nearly topples over the blonde statue ahead of her. Emily mouths, "What's going on?" while Ms. Val clears her throat.

"Brittni, why don't you take attendance while the girls stretch?" With that, mother walks away from daughter, leaving only stunned silence.

Emily's eyes dart between my tightly wound nemesis and myself. "So, you can mark us here."

Brittni appears to have super powers as her icy daggers transform to a fiery glare aimed at Emily. "I got it. Thanks." She stalks off with clenched teeth.

I expel my nervous energy, hoping Emily doesn't ask.

We shuffle to the other side of the room for stretches on the mat, neither speaking until we start our third butterfly stretch. Emily leans toward my side and smiles. "So, I gather it wasn't Bethany's fundraiser idea?"

You're Amazing

CHAPTER SIX

LENA

Nine in the morning, and I'm already exhausted. I peek into the pre-school room where Marshall's apparently forgotten about his "mommy's leaving" tantrum and is already racing for the trucks. Alex is in his class, and that leaves me without children for two hours. Two glorious hours.

A hot mocha with a half pump caramel and a trip to the ATM later, I take that caffeinated energy and decide grabbing a few groceries without the kids is the most exciting way I can spend my free time. As I navigate the cart through the narrow produce aisles, I spot a familiar face from my late teen years. Valerie Frost.

"Mrs. Frost? Hi. Lena Fiorello. Actually, I'm Lena Calloway now, but I used to babysit for you."

Her pastel blue eyes flash with recognition, and she smiles. "Of course. You were my favorite. If you're grown and married, that means I'm as old as I feel."

I twist my wedding ring. "I'm the one looking for a babysitter these days. I have two boys who keep me a lot busier than I remember you being when your daughter was young. Maybe I was a naïve teen, but you made motherhood look easy."

Her laugh is soft as she shakes her head. "Those times we called weren't because of meetings or work events. My husband called them my 'mental health breaks.' He was right." She chuckles again. "Now that Brittni's a teen, I should remind Dale about those respites."

Jazmin's rant regarding the younger Frost comes to mind. "I mentor teens. Those years don't sound any easier than the diaper and pacifier ones I'm drowning in now."

She nibbles on her lip for a moment. "You know, I teach dance at the Poise Academy, all levels. I have a few ladies that take a beginner class just to get out of the house."

Visions of me attempting to clog spring through my imagination. Sure beats bath time. "That sounds like fun. One of the girls I spend time with recently started dance at Poise. She even mentioned you. Jazmin West."

Valerie's smile widens. "Oh, that girl is a talent. I even invited her to join an advanced class for women. Jazmin has a lot of potential." She pauses to dig inside her purse, pulled out a white card, and offered it to me. "You do too, Lena. Please consider taking a class. First one is free. I remember well the season you're in. Do something that helps you remember you're more than spit-up and laundry."

The mere mention of those duties makes my palms sweat and mouth to go dry. "I'm so glad I saw you. A dance class sounds like a perfect...mental health break."

"Good for you. Who knows? Maybe you'll even pass Brittni or Jazmin in the halls."

Once the boys settle at home with lunch and Marshall goes down for a nap, I open my phone browser and search the URL listed on the business card. So many classes. Ballet. Hip-hop. Swing. Clogging. A beginner class I could actually go to if Bryce was home on time. With a quick text to verify he would be, I prance to my closet. *Need to find those clogs.*

I stand outside Poise Academy as the sun sets. Am I selfish to try something new? Guilt sticks to my ribs harder than my dinner. Pushing negative thoughts aside, I march to the front doors and sigh. "Okay, Calloway. Let's give this dance class a whirl."

"Ms. Lena? What are you doing here?" Jazmin stops in the hall before I can even shut the door.

I point to my knapsack. "Valerie Frost and I saw each other at the store. She encouraged me to try a class. I figured why not?" My voice rises higher the more I talk.

She nods. "Awesome. Which class? Hip-hop? Swing?"

I cough and smile. "Clogging. My cousin does it. She loves it, talks about it all the time. I thought it would be fun."

Jazmin raises her eyebrows. "I mean, if that's what you want, good for you."

I guess I can cross a clogging class off the list for possible Linked activities. "Hey, don't knock it until you've tried it."

"You sound like my grandmother. Well, I have to find my class. Do you need help?"

I look behind her and see the room directory. "No, thank you. Have a great class."

She flashes a peace sign. "Happy clogging."

You're Amazing

Twenty minutes later, I cringe when "Turkey in the Straw" starts for the third time. My right foot begins to move with a tap backwards and forward when the music stops.

Valerie isn't my instructor, but an all-business clogger named Helen rolls her dark brown eyes as she stops in front of me. "You're doing it wrong again. We start with the left foot, not the right. Then we do a double step by moving forward, then back."

The ten other beginners face me with looks ranging from grins and probable amusement to scowls that make me wonder if I'm killing their stage dreams. I take a deep breath. "This is a beginner class, right?"

Helen juts her nose toward the ceiling. "It doesn't mean we take the instructions lightly."

I glance at my feet, willing them to suddenly find coordination. "I'm trying."

Her lips form a thin, straight line as she turns on her heel and returns to the music. *Was that move a rock-step?*

Bless that Helen, she repeats the same steps for the rest of the time until I'm finally able to get that turkey out of the straw. My calves want to moo and I'm tempted to hide in the supply closet and nap so I have the energy to drive home and put the kids to bed.

Helen cups her hands around her mouth as we start for the exit. "We meet same time each week. If you think you could use a refresher of this lesson, we repeat Thursday mornings at ten. Good night."

I swallow hard, wondering why the woman didn't just call out my name for the last part of her announcement. I dump the clogs in my bag and decide I'll put my street shoes on as soon as I get out of the room.

A woman with a shoulder-length auburn hairstyle taps me so lightly that when I turn, I wonder if she did so by accident. She offers a warm smile. "Don't worry about Helen. She doesn't act like a drill sergeant every time. I'm Stacy."

I swerve over to a wooden bench on the side of the hall to change shoes and hopefully enjoy a chat with the red-haired clogger. "Thanks, Stacy. I'm Lena. I was beginning to think I was the only thing keeping you all from being on Broadway."

She giggles and takes a seat next to me. "I can always tell how her kids are behaving by her mood in dance. My guess is her high schooler got suspended again."

I drop a shoe. "Wow. Sounds stressful."

Stacy nods. "She lives on the street where my husband grew up. Not the best part of town."

Suddenly, Helen doesn't seem as much of a bully as a victim. "Wonder how she got into dance?"

Stacy shrugs. "She's a single mom. That's all I know." She stands. "I have to go. My husband, Jack, thinks our toddler should stay up so I can see her when I get home. If I run too late, it's pandemonium because Anna's overtired."

Haunting memories of the Great Juice Fiasco come to mind. "Right. Same here. I have two boys."

41

She flashes another smile. "It was nice to meet you. You'll come back, right?"

I glance to the side and notice Helen scurrying out, phone to her ear, face pinched. With my footwear on, I also stand and walk with Stacy to the door. "Yes, I'll see you next week."

Stacy's car is on the opposite side of the lot, so I wave and head to my vehicle. As I reach the row, Helen clicks off her phone and hits a button on her keys. Her door opens. *Should I approach her?* My overstretched muscles beg me to stand down. My heart challenges me to double my pace and reach her before she leaves. "Helen?"

She narrows her eyes. "I have to go. I didn't mean to be so critical."

I shake my head and put my hands on the top of the door, praying she doesn't get mad and try to shut it. "No, no, I'm not here to complain. I was going to tell you I'm sorry I wasn't very good tonight. Valerie encouraged me to try something new and this class sounded fun. I'll pick up that extra class so next week will be satisfying for everyone."

The lines in her forehead tighten. "You know Valerie? Please don't report me. I need this job."

The desperation in her voice nearly brings me to tears. "I used to babysit her daughter. I don't know her well. I promise I won't say anything. Why would I?" I chuckle and point at my legs. "This clogger has two left feet."

Her features soften. "You weren't that bad."

It's my turn to roll my eyes. "No need to lie for my sake."

She puts the keys in the ignition. "Okay. Maybe taking the repeat class isn't a terrible idea. Next week will be better."

I nod. "For both of us."

Her phone buzzes and she glances at the screen before facing me. Her forehead tightens again. "Right. Next week will be better for both of us."

You're Amazing

44

CHAPTER SEVEN

JAZMIN

As I reach the entrance to my new class, haunting piano music flows through the hall. It's a fast piece, at least for my skill level, but the tune grips my heart and doesn't let go. It's not a song, it's a story.

A shout from the center of the room snaps me back to reality. "Did you bring your pointe shoes?"

I look around and realize no one else is near me. "I'm sorry. Are you talking to me?"

The tall woman with a silver, thick bun on the top of her head turns to the other side of the room and points. I step inside the studio and see five other women stretching on the barre. They all have pointe shoes.

My heartbeat feels like it's trying to compete with the piano. "I forgot."

She gestures me toward her with a bony finger. "Ms. West, correct? Valerie told me you'd be joining us."

I extend my shaky hand, but she doesn't reciprocate. Her stern features render me speechless.

"You've been given an incredible opportunity most women clamor for and don't receive. Participation in this class sends a message that ballet is your passion, and you take it seriously. Forgetting pointe shoes screams you're a child with no business being here."

Every clipped word she throws is a punch to my gut.

She sighs. "Start stretching. We're working on *Mariage D'Amour.* Our recital is in December."

I nod, still frozen. *Run, girl, run. This class is over your head.*

The graceful bully slightly tilts her head. "Ms. West, were you waiting for me to walk you to the barre? This is not a child's class. Time to grow up."

I bite my bottom lip so hard I pierce skin, the metallic taste of blood in my mouth. "No, ma'am. I didn't catch your name."

She straightens, revealing flawless cheekbones even Beyoncé would envy. "Ms. Esmeralda." With that introduction, she claps her hands and gives her attention to the others. "Ladies, I have high expectations for this piece. Let's begin."

Ms. Esmeralda clicks her phone and the mesmerizing song begins. As I stretch, I watch the others, probably eight to ten years older than I am. Their pointe work is breathtaking. My shoes are home because I didn't get the blood and sweat removed.

This class? It looks like it will bring the blood, sweat, and the tears.

Two hours later, I text Mom and Grandma that I'm on my way home. It's tempting to add that I'm exhausted, humiliated and sore, but even my fingers don't have the energy. When Brittni sidles up next to me, I want to play dead.

Her smile looks like it was pasted on with Elmer's Glue. "Well, hello Jazmin. I don't get to see you now that you've been promoted. Everyone misses you."

My smile is as warm as an icy pond. "Thanks. With me gone, are you able to score any solos?"

Brittni's grin turns to a scowl. "With you promoted, are you feeling overwhelmed? If you don't mind me saying, you look beat." She turns up her nose. "And in need of a shower."

Lord, grant me patience. Now. "Brittni, we can play the insult game all night long. What do you want?"

She purses her lips and sizes me up. "I've seen dancers like you come and go. My mom praised and gave them high hopes. It didn't take long before they were overwhelmed and their dreams died."

I sigh and rub my temples. "I appreciate your concern."

Brittni zips her coat as she pushes on the heavy doors. "Don't say I didn't warn you." She walks through, barely leaving it open enough for me to exit before she stops and faces me, a grin growing the closer she approaches. "Oh, I almost forgot. Your friend? The poor one with rags for clothes and a sad excuse for a dance bag?"

Now I'm seething. My jaw locks and teeth grind. "Her name is Emily. And sometimes those who don't have a ton of money are the richest people around."

She pats her heart as if she's overcome by emotion. "Of course. She's rich in spirit."

My words are slow and tight. "What about her?"

Brittni's smile grows. "While you were promoted, Emily was demoted. She's back in beginner."

With that, she waves and races down the steps toward the parking lot leaving me sick. *I promised to help Emily. Is this my fault?* Sliding my phone out of my pocket, I shoot Emily a text.

Hey. You ok?

My phone dings within seconds. *Meh. Failing math.*

Aww. Sorry to hear that. How's dance?

Ugh. Worse.

Guilt seeps through my veins as I type. *Can I help?*

Brittni says you'd be too busy now that you're in advanced.

That princess loves to divide and conquer. *Since when do we listen to HER?*

The second I found out I'm back in a class with little girls.

CHAPTER EIGHT

LENA

The corners of Bryce's mouth turn up as soon as I enter our bedroom wearing my little black dress that only sees the light of day once a year or so. He fumbles with his cufflinks before giving up and making a beeline for me. "Let's forget A. J. 's wedding and stay right here." His husky voice exudes flirtation and fun as he wraps his arms around my waist.

I step back, but hold his hands. "No way, Calloway. We haven't been out, just the two of us, in months. I'm sick of wearing sweats. This dress needs attention."

He smirks. "So do I."

His dimples are hard to resist, but A. J. and Penny are friends from our church's small group. "Honey, we have to go." I lean in and plant a kiss on his cheek. "But remember, my parents are keeping the boys overnight."

Bryce pumps his first in the air. "God Bless Grandpa and Grandma."

Three hours later, Bryce and I stroll through the maroon and cream balloon arch and find our place settings not far from the band. When he pushes in my chair, Pastor and Cheri Wayson approach the table.

"Looks like we're having dinner with the Calloways." Cheri holds up her card to show her husband.

Pastor nods and helps her with her seat. "Excellent." He faces us. "Seems like yesterday we were at your wedding reception."

Nostalgia seems to lodge in my throat as I glance toward my husband, his adorable grin still triggering those dimples. I twist my ring. "Six years."

Cheri places the linen napkin on her lap. "And two beautiful boys later."

Before I can lock eyes with Bryce and offer a furtive wink to let him know I'm looking forward to a boy-less home later, an older couple from church, Chuck and Sally Lewis, take the last two places at our table.

Sally's heavy musk overwhelms as she fills her water glass and points to the appetizers across the room. "Chuck, they never serve dinner right away at these things. Get me some veggies and assorted cheeses so I don't feel faint."

Bryce's smile disappears as he clears his throat and rubs his nose.

Sally shakes her napkin as her beleaguered husband shuffles off. "Hello, Pastor, Cheri. And it's the Calloway family. Wasn't the wedding the loveliest?" Her tone nearly drips of maple syrup.

Cheri takes the bait. "It really was. I know when Penny turned twenty-five, she worried she'd never find anyone, but God had A.J. in mind all along."

Pastor, Bryce and I nod while Sally sips on her water. "He comes from a large family. I wonder if the newlyweds will follow suit."

I shrug, unsure how to make small talk with a woman who nearly put me in tears last year with her intrusive questions during a Vacation Bible School meeting.

Chuck returns, placing a small plate full of cheese, pepperoni, and cherry tomatoes in front of her. "The Beckmans said they saw the wedding party pull up in a limo."

Sally picks up a piece of pepperoni and grimaces. "Why did you get this? You know it's too greasy for me." She drops the slice with a huff, and then turns away from him to face me.

Now's a good time for the lead singer to announce the wedding party and stifle this opinionated woman. I crane my neck to the lead singer, but he's tuning his guitar. Nuts.

"So, Lena. It must be wonderful to have an evening out with your dashing husband."

I reach for the water pitcher and shoot Bryce a "help me." He starts a chat with Pastor Wayson. *Coward.* "We're excited to support the happy couple."

Sally smiles. "Of course. I talked to Penny at her shower and I don't think there was a more excited bride. She even transferred labs so she could work closer to the new house they bought. I don't understand her job, I think she tests blood samples." She shifts her chair closer. "Tell me, dear, what do you do?"

I hold tight to the water container. *Please Lord help me not drop it.* "I'm a wife and mom."

"That's an answer my generation would give. You're close to Penny's age. You must have a career, right? How about those direct sales businesses?" She tilts her head toward her husband. "Chuck says those are pyramid schemes but I bought a foundation that I love."

The water spills a little onto the tablecloth as I pour. I return the pitcher and place my shaky hands on my lap.

51

"The boys keep me pretty busy, and God provides through Bryce's work."

Cheri's eyes widen. Probably not her first awkward conversation with Sally. "Lena is one of our mentors with the Linked program. She does a fantastic job working with the middle school girls."

Sally sighs as she plays with a piece of cheese. "How nice. But Lena, what's your purpose? You can't gain any sense of self-worth with laundry and bringing treats to a youth event."

Drums break Sally's rhythm. Without answering, I focus on the band.

"Ladies and gentlemen, time to start this reception by introducing the wedding party!"

Thankfully, Sally turns her chair and starts clapping. Looks like she's moved on.

Bryce places his hand on mine and his breath near my ear causes the hair on my neck to stand. "You okay?"

I lace my fingers with his as the maid of honor and best man dance toward us. "I wish we could leave now."

His dimples return as he straightens and whispers, "What did she say that made you so saucy?"

I choke out a muted laugh. No boldness intended. I just want to go home.

A.J. and Penny shimmy through the balloon arch to cheers and whistles as we all stand. When they pass us, all I can envision is Penny in a lab coat making a difference. Then there's me, completely inadequate in this little black dress.

Bryce leans in. "Sure you're okay?"

I grip the chair to keep my balance and mouth "uh-huh" over the band's first notes. As the bride and groom begin their new life with their first dance, I consider what I offer our little family.

Laundry and meals.

You're Amazing

CHAPTER NINE

JAZMIN

I love when my weekend begins at our favorite coffee place, Mugs. Bethany, Hayley, Jade, and Emily meet me after school for assorted pumpkin-laced drinks. It seems like the hangout is full of Center Street students, but we find a booth and let the caffeine refill our energy.

Jade's the first to speak. "Who thinks they failed Wayson's test? I thought her having a boyfriend would make our studies easier, but I didn't know half the answers."

Hayley eyes her former frenemy. "I didn't think it was that hard. Did you study?"

Jade moves a wayward piece of hair away from her cat-green eyes. "No, I was counting on her making it easy. Lesson learned."

Bethany leans in like she's ready to share a government secret. "I think her neighbor boyfriend will propose by Christmas."

Hayley nods. "Thanksgiving."

Emily joins the guessing. "Same."

I take a sip of my pumpkin spice frappe, savoring the spices before offering my thoughts. "Sabrina would fail you all for gambling on her love life. Don't forget, she's not only our teacher, but a Linked mentor."

Emily sighs and plays with her phone. "Failing reminds me of dance class. I had my first one after returning to beginner. I'm the oldest, no contest."

You're Amazing

My sarcastic laugh breaks through the white noise around us. "I'm the youngest and the one Ms. Esmeralda seems to enjoy targeting with her criticism." Memories of my last practice come to mind where my bandaged feet screamed as loud as my instructor did.

Hayley never minces words. "Why do you two dance? Sounds like you hate it."

Good question. Dance was life, and I loved it. Lately, I feel like it's consumed my life, and somehow it's different. Not in a good way. "Hate's a strong word."

Emily puts her phone on the table and looks at me. "I'm ready to take you up on extra practice. Maybe we could have a session before our next Linked meeting? I know I'm not gifted or anything, but being demoted stinks."

Funny, because my promotion doesn't feel like a blessing no matter how many times Mom repeats it. "Sounds good. It doesn't matter if we're the best. The important part is to have fun. We'll get there, Emily." First, I need to convince myself.

Emily's the first to arrive an hour before our Linked meeting. As soon as I see her tattered bag, I think of Brittni and her rude comments. Thankfully, we don't have to deal with her for now.

She tightens her ponytail and jogs toward me. "Ready to help me return to a more age-appropriate class?"

I unravel a few gym mats and click my favorite ballet playlist on my phone. "Let's do this."

Emily listens to my instructions as I walk her through an advanced routine. She wobbles after her pirouette. "I'm not the most coordinated."

"No worries, pirouettes are new. It takes practice. Make sure you watch your arm placement."

She nods, and looks to the clock. "It's almost time for Linked. Thanks for helping me. Do you know what Linked is about?"

My stomach emits a level ten on my hunger scale. "No clue. I hope Mrs. Cheri brings donuts, though."

When we walk into the room, Lena's lifting plastic wrap off two pumpkin rolls. *This will do just fine.*

Lena smiles as she distributes plastic plates. "I finally remembered to bring the food I promised."

Bethany holds up a fork. "It's all good, Ms. Lena. You delivered some good stuff tonight. I could eat one roll myself."

Jade playfully shoves her aside. "This cream cheese goodness is my dinner. Stand in line."

Lena chuckles. "You girls know how to make someone feel special. Who knew all I had to do was bring food?"

Mrs. Cheri smiles as she places a canvas tote bag on the table. "Lena, you offer so much more than food. I hope you know that. In fact, our project this evening is designed to help us all remember our worth."

Emily grunts as she pitches her fork into her slice. "My dad was mad at me for sassing him and he said I was worth about two bucks on eBay."

Sabrina's eyes widen as she takes a seat. "I wish adults understood how important their words are."

We nod as we shovel the pumpkin dessert into our mouths. Mrs. Cheri continues to unpack the tote. There's construction paper, notebook paper, staplers and pens.

Hayley leans in. "Tell me this isn't a hard craft. I'm such a loser when it comes to art."

Mrs. Cheri drops the bag on the floor and faces us. "Girls, that's exactly what we're going to talk about tonight."

Jade, Emily, and Bethany exchange looks with raised eyebrows.

Hayley's voice is an octave higher. "You mean we're going to talk about how I'm a loser?"

Sabrina's giggle floats around us. "Not at all. When I was in middle school, we made slam books. They were awful. They were basically writing prompts passed around where we filled the blanks with insults." She holds up construction paper. "Instead, we'll create encouragement books. Mrs. Cheri wrote some sentences in each book. Create your cover, staple the pages together, write your name on the cover. Then, pass it around and we will fill your book with uplifting comments."

Cheri uses her maroon colored fingernail to point to a prompt. "I hear way too often from girls of all ages, even my age, self-deprecating remarks. You treat yourselves like junk, and God doesn't make trash. My prayer is that you read these answers over and over, along with the promises in the Bible. You all are worthy and more precious than all the jewels in the world."

Emily folds her hands against her chest. "How do you know that?"

Cheri hands her the supplies. "Because in heaven, God uses gold as pavement. If our most precious commodity on earth paves the road in heaven, you're pretty valuable to your Heavenly Father."

With that wisdom, we pick up our pens and begin.

I'm not an artist, but I figure I can't go wrong drawing a bouquet of flowers for my cover. It's tempting to scribble like a preschooler so I can fast forward to the prompts. Fifteen minutes later, I use my neatest handwriting for my name and pass my book to Jade. *Here goes nothing.*

Lena passes me her book where I see the prompts for the first time.

When I think of you, I smile because:

That's easy. I inhale the food she brings to Linked, so I reply, "You sacrifice your time to bring us great food."

Emily's book is also fun to answer. One of her prompts said, "The one thing that makes you so easy to love is that you never give up. You're so strong. I'm so glad you moved to Youngstown."

Jade. Now that's a doozy because I don't know her as well and she hasn't always been the kindest, especially with Hayley. *If your life became a movie, this actress should play you because…*

Hmmm. I need to pick someone with green eyes. Jade's last name is perfect because those emerald eyes pop. "Scarlet Johansson. You're gorgeous like she is and you could totally be one of the *Avengers*."

Mrs. Cheri announces we have five minutes before youth group starts. I'm working through Sabrina's, and then I'm done. The more I write, the happier I feel. Encouragement is contagious, just like my grandma always says.

Bethany taps my shoulder. "Jazmin, I have your book."

Resist the urge to grab it. "Oh, great. I think Emily has yours."

Beth glides over to Emily in seconds and has her hands on her book. "You're done, right, Em? I want to read mine."

I close Sabrina's and hand it off as if I'm chill about the whole thing. Glancing around as I sit down, no one's watching. Even the adults are reading their encouragements. I flip to the first page and find the first prompt.

You're the first person I want to: text in the morning. Have a frappe with. Look for at Linked because you have a great smile. The more I read, the more amazing I feel.

The three words I would use to describe you are: kind, fun, talented. Faithful, smart, beautiful. Hilarious, awesome, kind. The answers are all replies I'd never attach to my name. I sneak a peek at Jade. She swipes against the corner of her eye.

Sabrina stands. "I love this, and I'm going to keep mine close by so I can be reminded of how worthy I am, even when I don't feel awesome. I hope you do, too."

Emily turns her page sideways. "If I was old enough, I'd get this page tattooed on my arm."

Bethany grins. "Yaaass! That would be life."

There's a tight crease that suddenly appears on Mrs. Cheri's forehead. "How about for now we keep these positive words on paper?"

I rise with the rest of the group and hold my construction paper creation close to my chest. As we trek to the youth group area, I steal one more glance at a prompt. She's the best: Friend. Child of God. Dance Teacher. Dancer. Dancer.

These words feel like medicine to my aching feet and tired body. Before I join the other teens, I open my bag and place the book inside. *I'm going to read that before every dance class.* When I zip the backpack and place it to the side, I look up and notice a familiar face sitting across from me, her blonde tresses hang as she throws her head back in laughter.

What's Brittni Frost doing at youth group?

You're Amazing

CHAPTER TEN

LENA

The girls left for youth group twenty minutes ago, but I'm still in the Linked Room, throwing away plates and wrapping the last slice of pumpkin roll. Out of the corner of my eye is the encouragement book. The cover isn't anything fancy, but the mystery of what's written inside beckons. *Okay, just a little peek before I go home.*

The contents take my breath away. *You make me smile because: You sacrifice your time to bring us great food. You're a part of Linked even though you're super busy. You're a great prayer warrior. I love getting your texts every day.*

Cheri returns to the room and gasps. "Lena! I didn't know you were still here, this was my last job tonight, to turn the lights off. Everything okay?"

I nibble on my bottom lip. "This project was perfect. The girls needed encouragement. After reading a little, I realize how important these words are for me, too."

Cheri pulls out a chair and sits next to me. "We're never too old for affirmation. I remember the stage you're in. We were new to this church and received custody of Sabrina. I had no clue how to be a pastor's wife or a parent." She chuckles. "Still don't."

"Are you kidding? I'm pretty sure in your book a few of us wrote that you're a superhero."

She shakes her head. "If God had shown me as a little girl I would be a pastor's wife, I probably would have signed up to be a missionary in a remote jungle. I'm scared to death of disappointing people, and guess what? As leaders of this church, it happens all the time."

I sigh, remembering Sally from the reception and how it seemed my answers were unsatisfactory. "I disappointed Sally for not having a 'real' career like Penny."

Cheri offers a dismissive wave. "I wondered if you let her words bother you. God created each of us with a different plan. You aren't a cookie cutter. There's already a Penny, and she's great. But so is Lena Calloway."

That encouragement creates a second wind as I head home. Turning into the driveway, the house is lit up brighter than the airport at night. *The boys are definitely up.* The living room is most likely full of sugar highs and tantrums as I walk up the steps from the garage to the mudroom, then the encouragement book affirmations come to mind. *I'm great. I matter. I'm worth something.*

Then I enter the kitchen. The sink is full of dirty dishes. Our Bluetooth speaker blasts that shark song that teeters on the edge of my sanity, and no one is in the room with me to hear it. With each step toward the living room there's a crunching sound. "Ugh. Pretzels." With a deep breath I cross the kitchen threshold into the living room.

Bryce's bloodshot eyes find me first. "Mommy's home!"

Alex races at me like a linebacker with his eye on the football. He greets me with sticky hands and a runny nose, landing full force into my thigh. "We made art!"

I tousle his hair and glance around the room. *Please be paper and crayon art.* Two mini easels stand next to the couch. Paper that used to be white is clipped to them. One easel boasts a wet project with a lot of colors in a rainbow shape. The second is a huge blob of colors in a circle.

Marshall grins next to that project, waving with the same colors all over his palm.

"You two have been busy."

Bryce approaches me with slow steps. "They begged to paint. I'll clean up."

I run my hand through my day-three-without-shampoo hair. "It's okay. They love their creations. Let's get them ready for bed."

He tilts his head as if he's meeting me for the first time. "You feeling okay?" He brushes his painted hand over my forehead.

"Shocking, right? Let's celebrate the moment and not question it." I shoot a grin to assure him I'm not mad.

Bryce claps his hands and both boys focus his way. "Okay, soldiers. Bedtime. I need paintbrushes in the mud room sink. March on the count of three. One. Two."

Alex picks up his things and dashes away. "Three!"

Marshall, aware his brother has an unfair start, clenches the paintbrushes. "Twee!"

Thirty minutes later, the boys are tucked in and the easels are off to the side of the living room. I close the last lid of paint when Bryce enters the room. "Oh, Babe, I forgot to tell you. She said she tried to call you on your cell but it went straight to voicemail."

I turned to him. "She? Who called?"

His face flashes the same expression I had when the police gave me a ticket while driving Bryce's new car. "Your mom. She's coming to town for the weekend."

CHAPTER ELEVEN

JAZMIN

By the tight crease on grandma's forehead, she's doesn't look happy to find my head resting on my arm, surrounded by my school books. I straighten and shuffle my papers. "I'm not goofing off. Promise."

She shakes her head. "I know, Jazmin. But I am concerned at how tired you are lately. What's going on?"

Where do I begin? New dance class several times a week. Extra practices. Teaching before youth group so Emily can break out of the kiddie class. Dodging Brittni. "There's a lot going on. It should slow down once the recital is over."

Grandma pulls out a chair and makes herself comfortable. "Your eyes used to light up at the mention of recital. You just grimaced."

I scrunch my nose. *Is it that obvious?* "Ms. Esmeralda isn't like Ms. Elena."

She places her elbows on the table. "Do you miss the old studio? Or Ms. Elena?"

"Both. I enjoyed the class with Ms. Valerie before she promoted me. This class doesn't come easy even though I'm trying my best." My throat seizes as tears trickle down. "My best doesn't seem to be enough."

Mom enters, making a beeline for the coffee machine until she sees Gram and me at the table. "Whoa. Looks like a serious chat here." She slows her pace and redirects her route to the table.

"Jazmin's having trouble staying awake. This new class is too much for her."

Mom sits across from me. "What do you think?"

"I'm doing my best."

She exchanges glances with Grandma before focusing on me. "Do you think it's overwhelming?"

I shrug. "It's still new. I can do this."

Grandma surveys the books laid out across the table. "You're sure?"

I flip open my math notebook. "Yep."

The two stand and mom walks behind me and pats my shoulder. "That's my girl."

Nope. Not sure. Not sure at all.

The next afternoon, my mood's not any brighter when I start stretching in the small studio. The empty room appears full as I fight negative thoughts with each movement. *Your arm's too shaky. You're slouching. What kind of center work is this?* Every insult seems to be in Ms. Esmeralda's dreadful voice. My heartbeat increases when I hear footsteps approaching.

A blonde with a messy bun bobs through the doorway. Brittni. She drops her bag on the floor and walks toward me. "Hey."

I swallow and try to find my voice. And confidence. "Hi. Do you need the room? I came early to practice before class."

She shakes her head, and a blonde curl falls in the middle of her forehead. "No. I'm here for the same reason."

I shift position and extend my left leg on the bar, lifting my head to face her. "Really? You don't need practice." *And you know it.*

A sarcastic chuckle fills the room. "That's not what my mom says."

My leg nearly falls off the bar. "You're kidding. Your mom's really encouraging."

Brittni starts stretching on the bar, facing me. "To you. To the others. She's way harder on me. I even asked why. Mom said there can't be a hint of favoritism, so it's important to treat me like a dancer and not a daughter." As she lowers her head she mutters, "It's kind of stressful."

This explains so much. Mrs. Cheri often says "wounded people wound people." Brittni's a good dancer who can't please her own mother. "Can you switch classes?"

She shrugs. "I tried. Even volunteered to go with Emily to the lower class. Mom said it was nonsense, that by the end of the quarter she'll be back in our class."

Wow. Brittni doesn't hate Emily. And Emily won't be in the kiddie class much longer. "Can I help?"

Brittni looks up, eyes wide. "Why would you help me?"

I move to the mat and rest my hands on my toes. "Brittni, you're a good dancer. I know what it's like to second guess myself, and you shouldn't have to do that."

She joins me on the mat, but sits without stretching. "If only my mom would notice me. Say something good, you know?"

"Be thankful she isn't Ms. Esmeralda." I chuckle, but Brittni doesn't respond. "Your mom loves you. In a way, she's helping. My mom calls it 'building character.'"

Now Brittni giggles. "I hate when adults say that." She looks at the clock. "Ugh. Gotta go. Mom wants me to greet and take attendance. It's what I'm best at."

Wow. She has no confidence. God, what are You doing here? "Um, before you leave, can I ask a question?"

Brittni stands next to me, no longer giving chilly vibes as she picks up her bag. "I guess."

"You were at my youth group."

She snaps like my mom does when she's hungry. "That's not a question."

Lord, give me strength. "I'm getting to it. Would you mind if I prayed for you?"

CHAPTER TWELVE

LENA

Great. Grape jam on my wallet. I rub at it with one thumb as I fish a few twenties out with the other. "Here you go, Molly. Thanks again for coming on such short notice."

The college freshman reaches for the money with a wide smile. "No problem. Thanks for thinking of me, Mrs. Calloway. If you ever need housecleaning again, text me." She offers a wave and heads for the door as Bryce approaches from the outside. "Hey, Mr. Calloway."

Bryce greets Molly as they pass each other, and then he kisses me on the cheek. "What's the neighbor girl doing here?"

I clear my throat and look past my husband to note the shiny end tables. "Um, Molly lent me a hand today." I avoid eye contact and hope he doesn't press me further.

Bryce nods and places his laptop bag on the couch. He stops, focusing on the couch, before he faces me. "Lena, did you hire her to clean because your mom's coming?"

Ouch. "I mean, she did dust and vacuum, but because the house needed it." *She also scrubbed, polished, and ironed.*

Bryce shakes his head and pats the couch, taking a seat. When I join him, he sighs. "With two little boys, having Molly work on the house is the same as throwing money out the window. I know you're worried about your mom, but this is our home. It doesn't matter what she thinks."

Once I find the courage to look up into those kind eyes of his, my heart dances. "You're right. I get so nervous. It's like I'm twelve again. Thank you for reminding me."

He leans in for another kiss. "Honey, I've got your back. Your mom has a strong personality, but you forget we have secret weapons."

I tilt my head as I hear footsteps above. Seconds later, the boys are at the top of the staircase. Alex raises a ball and throws it down the stairs, which initiates a fit of giggles from Marshall.

Bryce whispers in my ear. "Your mom melts as soon as she sees her grandsons."

Three hours later, Mom opens the front door without knocking. Her thigh-high boots click on the faux brick steps as she rolls her suitcase to the side.

Bryce squeezes my hand before I let go and rush toward her with open arms. "Mom! You made good time. Did you have any trouble?"

She straightens and offers a hug that's as limp as I feel when I go to bed each night. "Hello, Lena. I guess if you count the potholes where I nearly lost the car, but no, it wasn't terrible." Her face brightens. "So, where are my babies?"

Bryce enters the foyer with the boys flanking his side. The three of them sport combed and parted hair, clean pants and shirts, and faces with no trace of dinner or dessert. "Hello, Millicent. No babies here."

Alex steps forward with an outstretched hand. "Hey, I mean hi, Grandma."

Mom bends down, her arms now look limber and flexible. "Alex? You've grown so much."

His laugh is the same as when I'm interrogating him and he doesn't want to get in trouble. "You, too." He walks into her hug.

Marshall jumps up and down. "Me too!" He jumps into the hug.

Mom stands, her gaze on them. "I'm so glad I can spend the weekend with these two. I hope I didn't interrupt any plans."

Bryce looks to the ceiling. "My boss was understanding and rescheduled our dinner meeting."

I reach for her suitcase. "Don't worry, Mom. We haven't seen you for a while. You're always welcome. Is there anything special you want to do?"

She looks around as she taps her finger on her chin. "I should have brought my sewing machine. Looks like someone needs new curtains."

The remark lands like a surprise missile. With a sharp breath I glance at Bryce, who stops staring at the ceiling and takes the luggage from me.

"Millicent, I'll take your things to the guest room. When I come back, we can catch up over coffee."

He winks at me as he heads upstairs. The boys follow him, and Mom sighs.

I smile. "So that sounds good, right?"

She sits on the end of the couch, then moves around as she keeps patting the cushions as she mutters, "Wow, this is lumpy." Once she finds a comfortable spot, she straightens. "Is Bryce making the coffee? Yours is usually nothing more than brown water."

This is going to be a long weekend.

Poor Bryce delivers the caffeine and even whips up a quick plate filled with cheese and crackers. He even offers to put the boys to bed.

Mom slaps her hands on her thighs. "Absolutely not. Let me. They see you all the time." She stands and treks to the stairs, leaving us no time to argue.

Bryce takes her place on the couch. "How are you holding up?"

My laugh is shaky, but at least I'm not sobbing. "My coffee is weak. The boys should have turtlenecks on so they don't catch pneumonia in this drafty house. She was just starting in on my sister's latest accomplishment when you arrived."

He looks to the stairs. I can't hear much noise, but Bryce stands. "Brenna may have a lot of degrees and frequent flier miles, but don't let your big sister get in your head."

I rise, and together we walk to the steps. "It's hard. Mom forgets Brenna's single. She has time to volunteer at the homeless shelter and have dinners with the mayor." I feel his hand on my back as we make our way to the boys' bathroom. "Thanks for reminding me there's no contest. My sister's life is hers, and it's great. I still wouldn't trade being married to you, having Alex and Marshall, even this drafty house."

We pause in the hall. There's definitely water running, but I can't tell if it's bath or sink flow. I can discern Alex's chatter as the faucet squeaks and the water stops. The door is open a crack.

"Then Mommy puts her hand in the water before she lets us get in. We play boats."

I shuffle a couple steps and find Alex climbing in the tub while Mom lifts Marshall and rests him on the bath mat across from his brother. Once they're both in, she reaches for her phone.

Alex's eyes widen. "No, Grandma. No phone when we're in the tub. Mommy says she'd never take her eyes off us."

My heartbeat returns to normal as she slides the phone out of reach and clears her throat. "Right. Sorry. I was checking for a work message, but your mother is right. What does she do after boats?"

Alex sighs. "Washes us and sings."

Marshall nods. "*Jesus Loves Me*. That's da best one."

I can feel the room temperature drop as Mom gives a perfunctory reply. Water splashes for a while before Mom speaks up, her tone more businesslike than grandmotherly. "Okay, tonight you two can sing to me. How about that? What do we do after washing?"

Alex's tone borders on squeaky. "Gee, Grandma, haven't you done a bath before? Dry us, but when Mommy does it, she uses the huge towel. She pretends she has to hug us for a good dry, but we know she just wants to hug us."

"Mmm, I see. Well, let's drain the water and move on."

I hold my breath as I watch the routine unfold. Bryce squeezes my shoulder and walks away, apparently satisfied they didn't drown on her watch.

"Grandma. You didn't hug. I thought all grandmas do."

I gasp, and Mom turns around, our eyes locking amidst a sea of regret.

CHAPTER THIRTEEN

JAZMIN

Emily nearly runs over me in the hallway when the seventh period bell rings. She balances herself by holding onto my shoulder, breathless. "Hey. Bethany and Hayley are going to Mugs and invited us. You in?"

Caffeine. That sounds glorious. "I wish. I have dance class. Again."

Emily straightens with a sigh. "You're always in class. Can you miss just this once? We never see you."

I quickly picture a race between Ms. Esmeralda and my family to determine who would be first to punish me for skipping. The thought is so unbearable I shake my head several times. "I can't. Sorry. I know I keep saying it, but once the recital is over, things will calm down." I hope.

Her shoulders hunch. "Okay. Don't be a stranger. It's not the same without you."

Emily's last words echo as I walk to Poise Academy, passing Mugs and all the happy students sipping their hot chocolate and peppermint mochas. I refuse to slow and see if my friends are inside. Knowing I'm trading giggles for a guaranteed tirade from Ms. Esmeralda intensifies my sadness. *Lord, I need some help here. I'm miserable* and *want to see my friends. I hate dreading dance. It never used to be this way. But dance is my passion.*

I kick at some dead leaves as the building comes to view. No answer to my prayer, at least nothing I can sense right away. Each step closer feels like my feet are encased in cement. As I bound the steps and open the heavy door, Ms. Lena's on the other side in the lobby, sitting on a bench.

"Ms. Lena? Do you have your clogging class?" I stroll over and sit beside her, wishing I could spend the evening chatting with her.

She pulls a pair of ballet shoes out of her bag. "I switched." Her smile widens as she gazes at the dusty rose satin.

"How come?"

Ms. Lena places the new shoes to her side. "A few reasons. One, I wasn't good. I tried to understand the terms and the timing, and I couldn't. I even went to extra classes. Two, it wasn't fun for me. If I'm taking classes to discover 'me' time, I don't want to hate the little time I have." She sighs and curls a couple strands of hair behind her ear. "I also don't want regrets. Life's too short."

Her words tempt me to dump my gym bag and run for Mugs. "What if your family thought you were destined for clogging but you didn't agree?"

She rests her elbows on her legs as she ponders my question. "If they truly loved me, I think they would want what's best. What I enjoy." She nudges me as she shuffles closer. "Jazmin, are you okay?"

My phone vibrates, a notification popping up that it's time for me to get to the classroom and start stretching. "I could use prayer."

Ms. Lena nods. "You've got it. Would you like me to pray now, or on my own?"

I glance around and notice a bit of traffic milling about in the lobby, but my heart warms at the idea of prayer. "Now would be great. Thanks."

She discreetly reaches for my hand and squeezes it as she closes her eyes. "Heavenly Father, we are here for such a short time, and we want to make every moment count for Your Kingdom. Direct Jazmin's steps, and give her peace as she waits. Thank You for bringing this amazing young woman into my life. In Christ's name, Amen."

"Amen." I open my eyes and lean in for a hug. "Thank you. I'm so glad you're here. Have a fun class."

Ms. Lena picks up her shoes and stands, giving me a wink. "I will. You, too."

With new courage, I breathe in slowly as I march to class. "I plan on it."

Unfortunately, Ms. Esmeralda isn't privy to Ms. Lena's prayer, and she's found a new level of angry as class begins. "Ladies, there is nothing, no-thing about your movement that shows you're ready for recital. We have fewer than three weeks. Arms should not be shaking."

I look heavenward as I hold the pose, counting the time before we're allowed progress to the jump. My ankles plead for mercy and my right hand decides it's time to unlock position. *Please, God. I want to get through the recital. Help me. This pointe work is exhausting.*

"No, no. Start over. We'll keep doing this until it's right."

I bite my bottom lip and gaze at my feet. The pain sends the same message my head does. *We're done here.* I lower myself to the ground and start to take off my shoes. My toes have a heartbeat.

Ms. Esmeralda strides over and bellows without glancing at me. "I did not say class was over. We're not even close to dismissal."

Forgive me, Jesus and Grandma, but I want to shove her right now. "I need to call home. Ms. Elena taught us that if our ankles get shaky and we aren't able to get over the box of our shoes in proper position, we need to work on building strength before moving forward with advanced techniques. I'm in pain."

Her face contorts like a villain in a Disney movie. "Pain is the process. Back to the beginning."

I fold my arms and narrow my gaze. "I'm not dancing anymore tonight."

Her cheeks turn versions of red I don't think even Kylie Jenner and her cosmetics have a name for. She bends down and is inches away as spittle hits my face. "That is for me to decide. Now, get back in line."

After she returns to her reigning position, I glance around and notice the other women are frozen in their standing positions, mouths agape. Their terror doesn't deter me as I gather my shoes, stand, limp to my bag, and drag myself to the door.

Ms. Esmeralda transforms to a furious gazelle as she glides to the entryway before I can, standing as a block to my exit. "Real dancers do not let pain deter them. If you leave this class, you will never return."

Ah, music to my ears. "I'm sorry, but I have to call my mom." Not waiting for a reply, I push past her. *Don't start to cry. Hold steady.* As I start my awkward trek to the lobby, a soft voice speaks from the hall.

"Jazmin. Could you use some help?"

You're Amazing

CHAPTER FOURTEEN

LENA

As soon as the boys spot the first snowflakes of the season, they're at the door ready to break out. I'm still sore from my first ballet class, but Marshall's so excited he's bouncing in place.

"Okay, we can go out for a little bit, but you have to wear your hats." I open the coat closet and reach for all the accessories.

"Can we make a snowman?" Alex pops up next to me.

A quick glance around the yard shows a scant half an inch. "I don't think there's enough snow yet. Maybe after dinner there will be." I turn to see his reaction, hoping there aren't tears.

"So, what can we do then?"

Good question. I think back on the things I wanted to do as a little girl. "Catch them on our tongue."

The two look at me like I spoke another language. Need to put a boy spin on it. "You mean you haven't played the winter race?"

They shake their heads, completely mesmerized.

I hand Alex his coat, hat, and gloves. "Then we have to play. We catch three snowflakes on our tongue, turn around three times, and then run to the porch. First one to touch the red chair wins."

Marshall struggles with his hat as he keeps track of how much faster Alex dresses. "I want to play!"

Alex zips his navy-blue coat. "I'm going to win."

After I help Marshall, I put on my winterwear and open the door to a cold blast of snow. "I don't know if I'll win, but I know I'll have fun."

They stare at me, as though my declaration makes enjoyment their new goal.

Alex waddles out first in an oversized ski jacket my sister bought for him. "Three snowflakes will be easy. It's snowing hard now!"

He's right. This weather keeps up and we'll be able to make a snowman tonight.

The race lasts ten minutes longer than I figured it would, and we follow up with snow angels. Their giggles take me back to my childhood where Brenna and I would run outside in hopes of forts and angels, only for mom to call us back in. "You'll catch a chill." I'm lost in thought when a flash of snow whizzes past.

"Marshall, you almost hit Mommy!"

I whip around as the two quickly drop their little ball creations. "Did someone throw a snowball at me?" I make sure they see my smile as I gather up some snow of my own.

"I did. It was me." Marshall bends over and tries to make another with his little gloved hands.

Alex lobs one that lands on my arm. He laughs so hard he falls back on the snow.

"Oh, it's on!" I use both hands to throw one at each kid.

Twenty minutes go by before I realize the three of us are soaked through. My sides hurt from laughing over missed attempts and funny faces. *Lord, my heart is full. Thank You for showing me this life is the only one for me.*

"Can we have hot chocolate now?" Alex's red cheeks could help planes land.

I grunt as I stand and trudge over to Marshall. "Absolutely. Let's get inside."

Once we shed the wet clothes and I microwave the drinks, I reach for my phone and realize there are missed notifications. Bryce is running late. Brenna asks if I have Christmas ideas for mom. Cheri reminds me it's my turn for childcare Sunday. Jazmin asks if she can come over. *Wait. She's never asked to visit.*

I quickly reply. *Jazmin, would love to have you. Do you need a ride?*

Her answer arrives in seconds. *Do you mind? I'm at home, but my mom and grandmother are working.*

My fingers haven't quite warmed up, so my texting is slow compared to Jazmin. *No problem. Everything okay?*

There's a lightning fast response. *Not really. I could use someone to talk to.*

Ten minutes later, the boys are in their car seats and we're off to Jazmin's. I can hear Bryce now, not pleased that I'm driving in the snow. It's a mile away, and the crews plowed. It's all good.

"Mommy, where are we going?" Alex kicks his feet against the back of my seat.

"We're picking up Jazmin, our friend from church. She's going to have dinner with us."

"What's for dinner?" Another kick.

I played in the snow so long, I forgot to defrost the meat. "I'll figure it out once we have Jazmin."

We pull into the short driveway and find her standing on the porch. She limps to the passenger side and slides in the seat. "Hi, Ms. Lena. Thanks so much for this."

I crane my neck as I back out of the driveway. "My pleasure. I'm glad you reached out. Your text sounded like you were having a bad day."

That's all the push she needs to release her pent-up feelings. Once she opens her mouth, she doesn't stop until the garage door is closed and we're bringing fast-food bags of chicken and waffle fries to the kitchen. The boys rush inside, most likely happy to be free from all the girl talk.

I place all the bags on the counter as Bryce greets the boys and the three take off to the living room, leaving us girls alone. "So, Jazmin, if I understand correctly, you were struggling in class and didn't think you could continue. When you tried to leave, the instructor said you could never return."

She nods and rests her leg on the chair across from her. "My ankle and foot arch aren't strong enough for the pointe work. My ankles still hurt. I hate the class, but it's so much more than Ms. Esmeralda. I'm not ready. But once my family finds out I walked out, I'm afraid they will make me go back. Mom thinks the last class ended early."

What a tough situation. "Have they seen you walk? You definitely look like you're hurting."

Jazmin shakes her head as she helps take containers out of the bags. "I sat until Grandma and Mom left for work."

I pat her back. "Oh, Jazmin. You know if this class doesn't work you're still a fantastic dancer. And Child of God."

She looks down to the floor and doesn't respond right away.

I reach for her shoulders. "Jazmin West, look at me and listen."

Her head rises until her tear-moist cheeks glisten in the light and she locks eyes with mine, her cheeks moist.

"Whatever that dance instructor said to you is not true. Don't let her words twist what's real about you. You're beautiful. Smart. You're a great friend."

Her voice is barely audible. "But I have no business being in a dance studio."

"That's a lie straight from the pit of hell. God gave you a gift. Don't stop dancing because one impossible-to-please teacher decided to target you."

Tears flow freely and hard enough that Jazmin gets the hiccups. Bryce walks into the kitchen, sees her upset, and leaves. I open my arms and she falls into my embrace, sobbing. I let her cry, stroking her hair. As she continues, my mind wanders back to a time when a girl I thought was a friend made fun of me and I ran home to my mom for comfort. When I tried to collapse into her arms, she stiffened.

"I'm sorry, Ms. Lena." Jazmin lifts her head and then nestles into my shirt again. My grip tightens as I gently touch her hair, overwhelmed with the opportunity to help when nurturing isn't in my genes.

You're Amazing

When Bryce tries to enter the room again, both Jazmin and I are crying.

CHAPTER FIFTEEN

JAZMIN

I've never seen so many tears shed as the last few days. There's my ankle pain, the love I felt when Ms. Lena let me cry all over her, and now, my Grandmother and mom at our kitchen table as I confess my last interaction with Ms. Esmeralda. The three of us sniffling and reaching for tissues.

Mom walks over to the extra chair I'm using to prop my leg. "Let's see that ankle." She unwraps the bandage with a gasp. "Lord, have mercy. Jazmin, this ankle is really swollen. We need to get you to the doctor."

Grandma paces the floor. "This is my fault. I went along with Valerie's suggestion to move Jazmin up without question. I didn't take time to learn the requirements or meet the teacher."

I wince as mom re-wraps. "Am I going to make the recital?"

The two freeze and put their hands on their hips. *Like mother, like daughter.*

I shrug. "What? What did I say?"

Mom picks up her phone. "You'll be lucky if you make it to school tomorrow without crutches. Let's get your ankle looked at before we talk about anything else."

Later that afternoon in the Urgent Care waiting room, I text my friends.

Emily's the first to reply. *Are you in a wheelchair? What's gonna happen?*

Emily loves to jump to conclusions. *No idea. But I wouldn't want to be Ms. Esmeralda when my mom shows up. No wheelchair. Mom thinks crutches.*

Her reply takes seconds. *You're not going to be in the recital, are you?*

The nurse calls my name before I can answer. The pit in my stomach grows. Before I follow the nurse, I shoot Em an answer. *I don't think a recital is happening.*

The doctor on call orders x-rays. After a two-minute study of the results, he looks to mom. "Lateral ankle sprain. Very common with dancers. I prescribe rest, ice, crutches for school, muscle exercises after a couple weeks, and six weeks without sports. If you need anything for pain, over-the-counter medication should do. Absolutely no dance until your doctor clears you."

I breathe in slowly, not sure how I'm supposed to feel.

On the ride home, Grandma turns around to make sure I still have my seat belt on. "How are you?"

I shrug and readjust my leg on the back seat, thinking if ever there's a time to get some food out of a situation, now is it. I'll milk this drama slowly. "Six weeks is a long time."

Her slow nod is the same pace as how she draws out, "Mmm-hmm. Do you think ice cream will soften the disappointment?"

Mom shoots me a look in the rearview mirror, but I ignore her.

"Grandma, you read my mind."

Word spreads quickly about my injury. Sabrina texts to not only check in since I stayed home to let the swelling go down, but let me know she'll bring me the homework I'm missing from her class. Even Brittni sends a snap to let me know she's sorry I'm hurt.

Two days after my urgent care visit, there's a light knock on the front door. Mom's tennis shoes scuffle against the kitchen tile as she heads to answer. Once Mom does, two sets of shoes shuffle closer. "Jazmin, Ms. Elena's here to see you."

I straighten on the couch, feeling warm and fuzzy as soon as I see my favorite teacher from my former dance studio. She glides in with a shopping bag that she rests on the floor next to me.

"Oh, Jazmin. I came as soon as Valerie told me. I got you a few things to help as you recover." She takes a seat as I pick up the bag.

"I love stuffed animals. And a necklace. Thank you, Ms. Elena." I hug the soft beagle. "What did Ms. Valerie tell you?"

"She feels terrible. Said she promoted you too soon. That she didn't ask about how long you've worked pointe. You were such a natural, she wanted you to be challenged. But never injured."

Ms. Valerie isn't the one I'm asking God to help me forgive. "Did she say anything about Ms. Esmeralda?"

Ms. Elena shakes her head. "No. I met her a few years ago at a fundraiser. Her methods aren't the same as mine, but she's classically trained. And a very graceful dancer."

I realize I'm choking my stuffed animal.

"Jazmin, is everything okay?"

I sigh and feel my lips tremble. "She didn't care that I was hurt. I had to leave the class against her will."

Ms. Elena's expression transforms as her breathing quickens and her mouth forms a tight, thin line. "If you had continued, there could have been a fracture."

Oh, I know. Go get her, Ms. Elena.

She stands, her gaze narrow. "I need to talk to your mom for a minute, but I'll be in touch. Make sure you follow orders."

I offer a mock salute, and she grins as she treks to the kitchen. The women speak in hushed tones, and I try to position myself so I can hear them without them knowing. All I catch are a few random words. Studio. Fire. Repairs. Impossible. Valerie. Esmeralda.

What's going on?

CHAPTER SIXTEEN

LENA

Dance has become a form of therapy. The beginner ballet class allows me not only to learn the terms, but also to move and express myself without words. I'm able to be Lena without letting go of the roles I cherish: wife and mom.

Emily runs up to me after my class ends. "Ms. Lena! Guess what? After the recital I'm moving back to the intermediate class." The glow on her face could light the night.

I drop my bag and offer our newest Linked member a hug. "Emily, that's fantastic. You practiced and didn't quit. Good for you."

She tosses her hair behind her shoulder. "It was tempting. I felt like such a failure when I was demoted. Especially when Jazmin was promoted. But then she gets hurt. She isn't even allowed to dance. I don't understand. I prayed for her. I knew that class was way harder than she was saying."

Wow. That's a God-talk that would take way longer than a hallway chat to explain. "I've talked a bit with her about this. Jazmin knows sometimes God allows struggles to grow us. And I'm learning our prayers are always answered, but not in the way we thought they would be. Shall we get coffee? I'd love to talk more if you're able."

Emily's shoulders slump. "I wish. My mom's picking me up. Raincheck?"

Thank You, God. I love these girls. "Absolutely. Don't worry about Jazmin. She's going to be okay."

Her phone beeps and she looks at the screen. "I gotta go. Mom's here. Thanks for listening. You're the best."

Jazmin and coffee are both on my mind as I head to the car, so I decide to grab a couple drinks at Mugs and visit my injured friend.

She answers the door while balancing on crutches. "Ms. Lena, what a surprise."

"Thought you could use some chocolate syrup and coffee."

Jazmin reaches for the cup and hobbles to the couch, gesturing me to follow. "Thanks for this. Prayer works miracles, but caffeine isn't half-bad, either." She winks.

I sit on the edge of the chair next to her and take a sip of my macchiato. "How are you feeling? Are you back to school?"

She nods. "Mom let me only miss one day so the swelling could go down. I can put a little weight on it, but not for long. Don't worry, if crawling the steps is the only way to reach the Linked meeting, I'll do it."

Gotta love a girl's dedication to ministry. "Hopefully your ankle will be a lot stronger by then. How about dance? Any updates?"

Jazmin reaches for a stuffed dog and holds it close to her chest. "No dancing until the new year. Ms. Valerie asked if I was interested in designing the invitations for the recital. Sounds like fun."

"When you're cleared to dance, will you be back in the same class?"

94

She shakes her head with enough force that her braids hit her face. "No way. I'll go back to Ms. Valerie's class. You really helped me that night letting me talk. Now that I know I'm done with Ms. Esmeralda's class, I have that peace you talked about."

Okay, Lord. These Linked girls make me want to have a daughter. "God has such an amazing plan for you. Whether you decide to become a professional ballerina or discover another talent to pursue, I know you'll be a world-changer."

Jazmin's grin intensifies my desire to have another baby. "Your prayers helped so much. I don't know what I'll do when I'm older, but there's one thing I'm sure of."

"What's that?"

She displays more of that beautiful smile. "I want to help young people like you do at Linked, and not be anything like Ms. Esmeralda."

Jazmin's comment stays with me even after I arrive home and put the boys to bed. Ms. Esmeralda's criticisms really messed with her confidence.

Just like your mother's words did to you when you were a child.

The thought's fleeting, but leaves a huge impact. "Okay God, but I'm an adult now."

The wound is still there. Will you trust Me enough to surrender it and let Me heal you?

Instead of traipsing to the living room and finding a show to binge on, I absorb the peace and quiet. Bryce is working late in his home office, and light snow dances

95

between the street lights and the front window. Using my index finger, I trace a cross on the glass. It's like the cold sensation connects with my past as memories long locked away loosen.

Mom's voice, tired and frustrated. *Girls, don't mark up the windows. I work two jobs, and I don't have time for extra cleaning here.*

Funny thing is, I only remember her telling us not to do stuff. I didn't recall her reasoning.

Looking at the outdoor lights, another flashback. *Lena, if I have to tell you one more time, I'll have you pay the electric bill. I can't afford for you to leave the television and the lamp on when you aren't in the room.*

My breathing slows and my stomach tightens. The snow triggers a time I fell on the ice as a ten-year-old. Mom, hearing my injured cry, met me at the door. Her response? *Lena, if I didn't cry over your father leaving, there certainly won't be tears over a little scrape.*

There's no time to process the scenes coming to mind. From Mom's angry vents when I was in elementary school to feeling emotionally paralyzed when she dismissed my high school accolades, the pain comes on like an avalanche.

I expel air and step away from the window. *God, I don't understand. These things happened so long ago. Why do you want me to deal with them?* Walking backwards, I stumble onto the couch, heart racing. One more decades-old scene plays out. I'm holding car keys, walking into the bank, where mom works. She's talking to her boss, Mr. Franklin, I think. Mom's back is to me, and he's focusing on her.

"Mr. Franklin, I have two daughters who need me. As much as I appreciate your recommendation, the position requires too many hours."

The man's expression darkens and his flat smile transforms to a mean smirk. "Millicent, the board considered you because they felt you were strong enough to carry the responsibilities." He turns on his heel. "I'll make sure they're aware that you are not. This was an opportunity of a lifetime and you squandered it."

Mom straightens. "Mr. Franklin, wait. Perhaps we can work something out."

His tone sounds dismissive. "No need. We'll find a worthier candidate."

Our pastor's wife's mantra comes to mind. Cheri says wounded people wound people plays out in the rejection Mom faced from my father, and at work. No wonder nothing was good enough. She didn't think she was adequate. The pain etched on her face as she turns toward me feels like repeated punches to my gut.

Okay, Lord. What do I do now?

You're Amazing

CHAPTER SEVENTEEN

JAZMIN

Mom's invitation to join her in the kitchen after dinner puts my brain on high alert. *Grades are good. Attitude has been decent. What's going on?*

Thanks to three weeks of light weight bearing on my ankle, I prance into the kitchen pain free. "Hey. You wanted to talk?"

She taps the chair next to her. "I just got off the phone with Ms. Elena." Her words are tentative, as if she's trying to choose what she wants to say.

My favorite instructor called? I plop into the chair with a wide smile. "You sound like there's news. Are the crews finally starting to build the new dance studio?"

Mom's mouth remains a thin line as she shakes her head. She speaks so softly I lean in to make sure I hear her. "Honey, Ms. Elena's not going to rebuild."

My hands grip the arm rest and I glance around the room, my voice rising. "What? She can't be serious. The only way I survived those classes at Poise Academy was knowing I would eventually return to Ms. Elena." I push against the table, rise, and huff around in circles. *Why isn't Ms. Elena rebuilding?*

Mom sighs but doesn't call me out for pushing the table. She lifts her coffee cup and takes a sip.

"Mom." My insides knot into a tight ball and lodge firmly in my throat. "She promised."

"Jazmin, sit down before you re-injure that foot. I'm not done. She wants to meet with us before the recital. We're going to Poise Academy and talk with Ms. Elena and Ms. Valerie." The corners of her mouth curve up. "Now I'm done."

"Wow. That doesn't make any sense. Ms. Elena didn't give any hint why she isn't rebuilding?"

She shrugs. "No, but let's hope for the best and not assume the worst. How's that sound?"

My imagination runs like a hamster on a wheel. Did Ms. Valerie threaten Elena? No, that doesn't seem like her. However, it does sound like that terrible Esmeralda… "It's hard, but I'll try."

"Do your best." She winks before sipping more of the drink.

Okay. Time to text the girls and update them. Maybe their theories won't be as outlandish as mine.

My black velvet dress sounds like corduroy rubbing against itself as Grandma, Mom, and I walk the main hall at Poise Academy. It's early enough we don't have crowds to dodge, but my recital butterflies take front row in my stomach. Even though I'm not dancing, nerves escalate as our appointment time with Ms. Elena approaches.

Mom fixes the button on her coat collar before opening the office door. "Now, Jazmin, no matter what anyone says in this meeting, you're to be respectful. Understand?"

Now would not be a good time to roll my eyes. "Got it."

Ms. Elena and Ms. Valerie stand as soon as we enter the conference room. There's a long, oval wooden table and swivel chairs for everyone.

Once we sit, Ms. Elena smiles and rests her arms on the table. "Ladies, thank you. I wish we had more time, but I know Ms. Valerie has a busy night ahead of her."

It's challenging to sit like a lady when my dress tag swiping my neck makes me want to itch. "Why aren't you rebuilding?"

Grandma and Mom narrow their eyes. They want me to show respect. No one said I can't be curious.

Ms. Elena's extra-large hoop earrings swing as she speaks. "Jazmin, you were a huge motivator in why I'm choosing this direction for my life—"

Mom straightens in the chair and points her index finger in my direction. "I apologize for whatever Jazmin has done. We love you and your studio."

Ms. Valerie's eyes rove from Ms. Elena to my mom.

Ms. Elena's silky black hair catches on an earring. "Oh, Ms. West, that's not it. Jazmin is a dream student. This season, I couldn't teach because of all the insurance and banking meetings. I realized that I don't love the responsibilities an administrator has."

Ms. Valerie clears her throat. "And this season has taught me a lot. There's so much I could have done better as an instructor, as an administrator." She catches her breath. "As a mom."

This is about Brittni and me? "I don't understand."

Ms. Elena moves her chair closer to the table, her voice soft and steady. "I am the new co-owner of Poise Academy. Valerie retains her investment, but her desire is to handle the business end. She will arrange the classes, bill students, promote the place."

Grandma and I lock eyes and she demonstrates her "mind blown" gesture. That makes two of us.

Mom focuses on the new co-owner. "What about you?"

"I'll return to teaching after Christmas break, taking Valerie's classes." She looks to her new partner. "And I'll co-instruct with Ms. Esmeralda. We'll make sure she offers her best classical training in an empowering way."

There's a knock on the door, and it opens, revealing Brittni looking around the room before she spots her mother. "Excuse me. Mom, the dancers from Intermediate Youth are here."

Valerie jumps up. "Thanks, Honey." She starts toward the threshold, but stops to face Elena. "Can I announce the latest news? I'd love to be the first to tell her."

Elena nods, the hoops wag back and forth. "Absolutely. You're the only one who should say it."

I crook my eyebrows as I glance at Brittni, who shrugs.

Ms. Valerie wastes no time reaching her daughter. "Brittni, Elena and I also want to use the great talent we have at Poise for different activities. If you're interested, we'd like you to become the new lead teacher for Pre-School, all classes."

Brittni's eyes widen and she rushes into her mom's arms. "Of course! I'd love to help. Thank you both so much." She chokes on her words, trying to regain composure.

I stand and offer my hand to the newest teacher. "Congratulations, Brittni. You're going to be fantastic."

She bypasses the handshake and wraps her arms around me for a hug. "Will you help?"

Grandma does another "mind blown" gesture. Wow, former mean girl and I have come full circle.

I step back, glancing toward Ms. Elena, before facing Brittni. "I'd love to."

Ms. Valerie opens the door and leans against it. "Jazmin, I apologize for the experience you had here. It's my fault you were hurt and doubted your abilities."

There's no need to look to my family for guidance. I shake my head. "It was a learning experience for everyone. I should have spoken up about being overwhelmed."

Ms. Elena joins our little circle. "The blessing is you'll be able to dance this semester. We're really excited about all the possibilities with this new arrangement. Once the recital is over, it will be time for new beginnings."

Brittni glances at the wall clock. "Speaking of recitals…"

Mom stands and shoos them out. "Yes, you ladies need to go." She winks at Brittni. "Break a leg."

My blonde friend grins as she reaches for her mom's arm. Valerie looks down, smiles, and grasps her daughter's hand as they head to the dressing room.

Ms. Elena tilts her head. "They asked me to hand out programs. Jazmin, want to help?"

Suddenly, the dress doesn't seem such a bother.

CHAPTER EIGHTEEN

LENA

Bryce extends his hand, palm up, so he can take my cell. "Sweetheart, you don't have a place for your phone with your tutu and tights. If your mother texts, I'll wave so you know."

I hand my cell over and take a deep breath. "What was I thinking inviting her to my recital? I'm a newbie, adult ballet dancer. She balks when I tell her about the Sunday school Christmas play the boys are in."

He squeezes my hand and slides my phone into his pocket. "Lena, you obeyed God. You felt prompted to tell her about tonight and make sure she knew she was welcome. The rest is up to your mom."

Not comforting. I look past my little family and spot Jazmin, practically glowing as she hands out programs. "I need to go backstage." I kiss him, and then the boys on their cheeks. "I'll see you all soon."

Marshall throws an air kiss. "Bye, Mama!"

Before I run, I look Bryce straight in the eye. "Don't feel the need to take pictures."

"No guarantees. Go get 'em."

The path to the dressing room is full of families ready to support their dancers. My stomach is as knotted as it was when I was in the fifth grade when I just missed placing in the top five in the spelling bee. F-O-U-R-G-I-V-E hangs like an albatross over my heart even as I push on the doors. Mom's disappointment in my ironic error floods back. *Maybe it's best she's not here.*

When Emily dances across the room and grabs my hands, she snaps me out of the past. "Ms. Lena! Can you believe it?"

I blink several times, trying to focus. "Believe what?"

She taps her phone, opens an app, and produces a live feed of the auditorium, courtesy of Jade. The seats are full of grandparents, parents, spouses, significant others and friends. "This is way more people than when I danced in Akron."

Maybe some of her excitement will rub off on me. "Is your mom here?"

Emily plays with a loose ringlet near her ear. "No, she had to work."

I reach to comfort her, but notice she's still grinning. "Is anyone else from your family here?"

Her smile doesn't dim as she shakes her head. "Guess who is, though?"

I shrug, positioning myself so I can see how my hair and makeup look in the tall mirrors against the wall. "No idea."

"Everyone from Linked. Jazmin was right, that group is family."

Peace floods my rejected heart as soon as Emily shares that wisdom. "Thank you, Emily, for reminding me. I hope you girls know the adults feel the same way as you do. I wouldn't trade the love we have for each other for anything."

Ms. Valerie scurries through, snapping her fingers. "Five minutes! We start pre-school in five."

Emily gives a quick hug. "Good luck."

The other dancers in my class gather near the curtain edge to watch the younger performers. Alex's laughter rings out above the music when a little girl decides to pull on another's tutu. Emily leads her class in grace as they dance to a medley of Christmas songs. My former clogging class has all the right moves for *It's Beginning to Look a Lot Like Christmas.*

Brittni Frost taps me on the shoulder as the cloggers take a bow. "Ms. Lena, adult beginner ballet is after advanced clogger. My mom wants you all to stretch one last time."

Ten minutes later, we take our positions on stage. My heartbeat competes with the music and blood pounds into my ears. As soon as Tony Bennett's smooth voice belts out the first notes to *My Favorite Things,* my feet commandeer the rest of my body and lead the steps. Each movement becomes more fluid than the last as I stand taller. The pasted grin I started with transforms into a real smile. *I'm doing it. And I'm having fun.*

"Hi, Mama!" Even Marshall's outburst during our final bow doesn't take away the exhilaration of trying something new and finding a little "me" time. It's only when I rise that I dare look into the audience.

The college girl next to me, Laney, speaks through her smile. "I can't see anyone. These lights are too bright."

"They are quite blinding." And perhaps saving me from seeing who isn't in the audience. There's no time to linger, because Ms. Esmeralda thanks us for our dance and announces beginner hip-hop is ready to show us their holiday moves. "The recital is almost over. Let's watch from the sidelines. Who knows? Maybe we'll find loved ones while watching from there."

Bryce and the kids flank my side with a beautiful bouquet of roses as soon as Ms. Valerie closes out the show. "Lena, you were fantastic. A natural. I'm so glad you did this. I knew you were an amazing wife and mom. Now I know another role you're great at."

"That means a lot. Thank you for loving me through my insecurities and exhaustion." I fumble with the cellophane from the flowers. "She isn't here, is she?"

He bites his bottom lip.

I lift the roses to my nostrils and inhale, drinking in the soft, romantic fragrance. "Babe, it's okay. She's doing the best she can, and I have two wonderful families here."

Alex shoves his lip out in an adorable pout. "Two families?"

I tousle his hair. "Of course, Daddy, you and Marshall are the first family. Then there is my church family, the girls and women from Linked. They're all here." I wave at Cheri, who is part of a circle talking to Jazmin. When she waves back, I feel loved from head to toe.

"Do you mind if I talk to them? Then maybe we can go out for i-c-e c-r-e-a-m."

Alex's eyes brighten. "Can we Dad?"

Bryce and I look at our oldest. "How do you know what Mommy spelled?"

He nudges Marshall. "I don't. But anytime you spell, it's always something good for us."

Once we determine ice cream is on the agenda, and hubby returns my phone, I jog over to the Linked crew. Jazmin and Emily both have bouquets with balloons.

Cheri's the first to hug. "Lena, you were excellent. I'm so proud of you for trying something new."

"I wasn't sure if I could do it, but I'm so glad I tried. I'm not the dance master Jazmin is, but I had fun."

Jazmin hears her name and looks up before walking over. "What was that you said?"

I dodge the balloons that keep blocking my face. "I told Mrs. Cheri what a talented dancer you are."

She smiles. "Stop, you're being too kind." Then she laughs. "You can go ahead. My ego likes this."

Sabrina slides closer to us, her boyfriend beside her. "These Linked dancers have some mad skills."

Bethany ducks under the balloon. "Maybe you two could take lessons. You know, for the wedding."

I stifle a laugh as Sabrina starts to cough. Bethany giggles and mouths to Jazmin, *Mission accomplished.* Before I can think of a reply, my phone vibrates.

Sorry I couldn't make your little program. I had to work. I bet you did great. Love, Mom.

You're Amazing

CHAPTER NINETEEN

JAZMIN

Hayley and Bethany reach for my hands as soon as I open the front door and pull me across the threshold to the outdoors.

I shake free and shiver. "Can I get my coat? The Linked party won't start without us."

Hayley raises her eyebrows. "Maybe not, but my mom might drive away if we don't head to the car."

The two return to the vehicle while I go back inside to get my things. Mom and Grandma are still at work, so my pace is almost a jog thinking about the pizza and cookies waiting for us.

Once buckled inside the back seat, Hayley nudges me. "How's the ankle?"

"It's all good. I stood and handed out programs for the recital and I was fine. I haven't tried to dance, though."

Bethany leans in toward us. "Yeah, Emily mentioned something going on at your dance place. What's that all about?"

Hayley's mom locks eyes with mine in the rearview mirror before I look to my friends and sigh. "It's crazy. Ms. Elena and Valerie co-own Poise Academy. Ms. Valerie plans to handle the business part, and Ms. Elena will dance and work with the other instructors." I giggle. "Including keeping Ms. Esmeralda in line."

Bethany falls back in the seat. "Wow. That's a lot of drama."

My stomach growls. *Pizza's coming. Just hang on fifteen more minutes.* "There's more. Brittni will be a teacher. Her and her mom are talking more and seem closer."

Hayley nods. "And Emily said Brittni's been really nice. She's even going to come to Linked."

I ignore the next wave of hunger pangs. "You know, our circle has really grown. It was the three of us when Linked started. Jade was there, but she didn't love it. Now Jade hangs out with us, and so does Emily. It's awesome that Brittni's joining, too. Maybe by high school there will be a huge group of us."

Hayley mumbles in agreement and pulls out her phone, texting away.

Bethany looks as if she's holding her breath. I ask if she's okay, but she turns toward the window and blows on the glass. She finishes the ride sliding her finger in circles against the steam, not saying a word.

Tomato sauce and pepperoni aroma fill the church's upstairs. Ms. Cheri, Lena, and Sabrina hung Christmas lights and have music playing. Once we turn the corner to the Linked room, we can see the Christmas tree is full of pictures of us throughout the year.

"Merry Christmas, girls! I hope you came hungry." Mrs. Cheri greets us with big hugs.

Bethany wastes no time reaching the pizza table. "Are you kidding? I could eat everything on this table."

I race over and give her a nudge. "Not if I get to a slice first."

Hayley rolls her eyes. "Amateurs. Anyone who loves a good Christmas party knows the cookies are where to spend your time."

Sabrina joins us and places a plate of pizzelles and biscotti down on the buffet table Cheri created. "Hayley, you're a girl after my own heart. Here's my contribution. Can't have an event in Youngstown without Italian treats, am I right?"

Mrs. Cheri asks us to wait for everyone to arrive before we enjoy the food. Once seated, she holds up her encouragement book. "I thought while we eat, I'd ask if anyone reads their book on a regular basis."

Mine is on my nightstand, edges crumpled from daily use. "I had mine in my dance bag, but now that I'm not active, I read it before I go to bed."

Jade holds her copy up. "Mine is in my backpack. I could lose all my school books and not care." She holds the book to her chest. "But this? It's a treasure. Thank you everyone for the kind words you wrote."

Hayley glances at her former enemy. "Jade's right. I didn't know how much I meant to all of you until I read your entries."

Emily nods. "Same."

Brittni raises her hand. "I missed that meeting. Maybe we can do this again so I can have one?"

Lena reaches in for a side-hug. "Absolutely. We're so glad you're here."

When it's silent for a moment, I take a bite out of my pizza and hear some slurping noises that's probably Emily gulping one of the bottled waters Mrs. Cheri labeled as "Melted Snowmen." A new hiccup-like sound erupts next to me. I turn to find Bethany in tears.

Mrs. Cheri notices my friend's distress at the same time. She jumps up to find a tissue, and hands it to Bethany, rubbing her back. "Sweetheart, what's wrong? Is it the encouragement books?"

She shakes her head, her high ponytail swings back and forth. "No. I love mine."

Hayley and I shift our chairs so we're facing Bethany.

Mrs. Cheri's voice soothes as she gently probes the situation. "Is something going on at home?"

Bethany lets out a strangled sob. The rest of us stare, feeling helpless.

Our pastor's wife turns to her niece, but more like adopted daughter. "Sabrina, can you get Bethy another water?"

Sabrina smiles as she recalls the childhood name for Bethany when Pastor and Cheri used to babysit. "Sure thing."

Although I'm still hungry, Bethany's anguish is stronger than my appetite. We wait as Bethany sips on her drink and blows her nose. Mrs. Cheri keeps rubbing her back.

Bethany takes a few deep breaths and offers a shaky laugh. "Sorry guys, way to party, right?" She sobers, and turns to Mrs. Cheri. "I found out the house we rent isn't being renewed. The owners want to sell."

Jade tilts her head and scrunches her nose. "That's what you're crying about? There's like hundreds of rentals in the area."

I roll my eyes and scowl. "I think Bethany has more to say."

My friend nods. "My dad texted me before the party. He thinks he found a house in Poland. He was really excited. Even has a pool."

Although Jade tries to whisper, I still hear her. "I don't understand how this is so upsetting."

Bethany sniffles and takes another drink. "I would have to change school districts. We could still come here for church and Linked, but my parents said it would be too hard to drive me from Poland to Youngstown and then to their jobs."

The reality hits me as hard as those tacos I bought at the fair. "Wait. We won't be going to school together?"

You're Amazing

CHAPTER TWENTY

LENA

Seeing most of our Linked girls in tears isn't how I'd pictured our Christmas party, but ten minutes after Bethany shared her possible switch to a different school district, I'm still passing out tissues.

As always, Cheri leads us through the middle school crisis with grace. She does such a great job rubbing Bethany's back that I'm tempted to ask if I can be next in line for some much-needed tension relief. Once Cheri finishes the massage, she returns to her chair and addresses us. "Girls, there is nothing that surprises God. Not one thing." She faces Bethany. "Honey, if you have to change schools, He will be with you. And we will be, too. Just like you said, you would still be a part of this church. You'd still see all of us."

Hayley and Jazmin take a cue from Cheri's positive attitude and nod. Jazmin lowers her pizza to her plate. "We could text or Facetime every day. This can work."

Hayley's tone doesn't sound as confident, but she's trying. "Absolutely. Besides, you said maybe. Nothing's definite. Who knows? Maybe you'll stay in Youngstown."

Bethany seems to consider this and the corners of her mouth lift. "Thanks, everyone. You're right. Let's get back to the party before youth group starts. Okay?"

Just as she says "party," there's a knock outside the room. It's our teacher, mentor, and friend Sabrina's boyfriend, her neighbor from childhood. Charlie Shell. He pokes his head in as he pushes his black-rimmed glasses up his nose. "Is it okay if a guy joins the party?"

Sabrina stands, but doesn't move. She opens her mouth, but doesn't speak. Her hands are on her hips as she tilts her head and gazes his way.

Jade decides to start with the questions Sabrina is probably trying to ask. "What are you doing here? Don't you work at the college?"

He takes a couple tentative steps forward. "I do." He chuckles and glances Cheri's way. "I brought a mocha for Sabrina."

I'm as confused as Jade, but I know better than to interrupt.

Jade utters a word, but Mrs. Cheri steps in. "Jade, let Charlie speak."

Charlie thrusts the holiday-colored cup toward Sabrina. "Here. I wanted you to have this."

Sabrina grips the sleeve. "Thanks." She raises her eyebrows and shakes the cup. There's no liquid inside. But her moving the cup makes a sound that reveals something is inside. "What's in here?"

She starts to open the lid, but Charlie stops her when he gets on one knee.

Brittni gasps.

I glance at Cheri, who nods.

Sabrina puts her hand over her mouth, her beautiful blue eyes wide.

"I asked Pastor and Cheri about this and if it was okay to ask here. I know how much the people in this room mean to you." He clears his throat. "Sabrina Wayson, I have loved you since the day you moved into your aunt and uncle's house. Will you marry me?"

We focus on Sabrina. Charlie takes the cup, turns it upside down, and a gorgeous ring falls into his palm.

Sabrina uncovers her mouth. "Oh, Charlie. I love you, too. You had my heart the first time you bought me a mocha. Yes. I want to be your wife."

I'm still whistling when I close the garage door and walk up the steps to the mudroom. When I turn the lights on in the kitchen, I notice how quiet it is downstairs. The kitchen sink is empty. The counter sparkles. Most of all, I don't hear two little boys running around like wild animals. "Bryce?"

I trek to the living room where there is soft piano music, but nothing about a baby shark or anything else pre-school related. The candlelight gives me the vision to see Bryce on the couch, waiting.

"What is this? What happened to the boys?" My voice squeaks out of excitement and curiosity as I sit beside him.

He leans in for a kiss, and then produces a small container. "Juice box? It's all I could find for a fancy drink."

I giggle and push the straw through, and we clink boxes. "Cheers. Are the boys in bed?"

Bryce nods. "I've been praying. One of the things God showed me was I've been wrong to keep the boys up when you go out, since you're with them all the time. I thought you deserved a night off from the bedtime routine. Is that okay?"

I put the drink down on the end table and wrap my arms around his neck. "You are amazing. Thank you. This is perfect."

His shoulders relax. "Oh, good. I didn't want to mess this up. I did want to talk to you a little bit. There's something I feel bad about."

I shift my upper body so I'm resting on his chest. "What? Did you get a speeding ticket?"

Bryce taps my arm. "Funny. No, it's about your mom."

I lift my head.

He reaches for my hand and squeezes it. "I wish she had seen you dance. After that text, she didn't even ask about it when you called her. Life just goes on. I feel like you get left behind."

What a sweet, sweet man you have given me, Lord. "Only if I choose to see it that way. The girls from Linked really taught me a lot. Emily was alone at the recital, but she didn't have that perspective. When her mother couldn't attend, Emily still believed family was there because Linked members came. My mom does her best. There was a lot against her when she was raising us, but she did it." I return to rest on him again. "I think I turned out pretty good."

"I definitely agree with that assessment." He kisses the top of my head. "So, you're okay that the kids and I were the only ones that watched your recital?"

"Absolutely. Seeing the three of you there really blessed me." Thinking about blessing reminds me of Sabrina and Charlie. "Oh, guess what happened at the Linked party?"

He clicks his tongue for a moment. "Hmm. Jazmin and Bethany fought over the pizza?"

"Yes, but that's not all. Charlie Shell surprised Sabrina. With a proposal."

My head falls to the couch cushion as Bryce jumps. "Get out! So there will be another wedding where we could sit by that nosy Sally woman?"

I push myself up to a sitting position. "I don't know about that, but if we have to sit by her, I promise you her words won't get to me. I love my life and what I do every day—it's pretty amazing."

IF YOU LOVED *YOU'RE AMAZING*:

It would mean a lot if you would leave a review on Amazon and Goodreads. The more reviews a book has, the more publicity it receives on Amazon.

A review can be as short as "I really liked it!" If you aren't sure what to write, you can share a couple things that stood out to you, as long as you don't give the plot away. If you know us "in real life," don't mention that. Thank you for taking the time to share your thoughts and to help us get this important message out to girls of all ages.

THANK YOU!

One thing we're learned in our own journey is that adults can have great intentions and still cause pain. Ms. Esmeralda was passionate about her work, and Millicent was doing her very best as a single mom who eventually poured her hurt into her work. The messages that Jazmin and Lena received was they weren't good enough or worthy.

If that's something that stirs within you, surrender that lie! The truth is our Heavenly Father doesn't create junk. You are a masterpiece on your very worst day.

Hannah and I appreciate the time you took to read. If you haven't read *You're Beautiful*, Hayley and Sabrina's story, please do. We believe it will encourage you.

Surrendering
Stinkin' Thinkin'

You're Beautiful---Hayley Atkinson
withdraws from her friends and new opportunities
with the new mentoring group, Linked, after she is
told a lie that she believes is true about herself.
Sabrina Wayson is a mentor in Linked who feels
she can't encourage girls because she's struggling
as much as they are. Can they surrender the lies
and find freedom?

You're Amazing---Jazmin has always been a natural with dance, and now that she's in junior high, she's been promoted to an advanced group with older girls. For the first time, her favorite activity isn't easy, and she feels left out. Lena enjoyed going out with friends, but after getting married and having young children, she doesn't get invited out much anymore, and she finds motherhood exhausting. Can these two members of Linked let go of their frustration and realize how cherished they are?

You're Brilliant---Bethany has a lot of changes in her life as a new teenager, but she decides to tackle it with her offbeat humor. No one laughs with her, and even worse, her classmates abandon her, making Bethany feel rejected. Mrs. Cheri is a pastor's wife who loves her life, but new commitments have her overwhelmed. A joke aimed at her goes straight to her heart, and she's convinced she's not good at anything she's been asked to do. Can these two stop believing lies about themselves and embrace the changes in their life with laughter and grace?

First Look Just for You!
Sneak Peek of *You're Brilliant*

CHAPTER ONE
BETHANY TUTTLE

One glimpse at the sprawling Boardman Valley High School campus and my throat starts to close up. It's a fortress. There's even an attached brick circular amphitheater to house the enormous drama and musical talent the Youngstown suburb is known for.

The morning crowd travels to the entrance. I'm trapped in the middle of the swarm, moving with the wave of peers, my anxiety escalating with each step.

What am I doing here? Oh, right. My parents moved and this is the closest school district. Where I know no one.

A boy with a head of curls wearing a Saturday Night Live shirt bumps into me. "Hey, tourist. If you don't know where you're going, step aside."

"Sorry. Did my fanny pack give me away?" I smile at my attempt at humor, but no one chuckles or even looks in my direction. There's so much movement. "Say, are we students or cattle?" My voice rises above the fray, but I sound like a squeaky kid.

"Keep mooo---ving funny girl." The tall blonde surrounded by three girls mimicking her every move, throws her head back and laughs. Her minions follow her lead and they're giggling with her.

I'm not as agile as my friend Jazmin, but I've got stealth working for me. With a few duck and weaves, I exit the throng of people and slam against the wall next to the office.

A slim, tall girl with shiny, straight brown hair is about to approach the receptionist when she looks my way and tilts her head. "Are you Bethany Tuttle?"

I raise my eyebrows. How does she know my name?

She gestures me forward. "C'mon. I'm KJ Curry. I'm the student council rep the vice-principal lassoed into keeping you corralled." Her expression is sober for about a second before she breaks into a chuckle.

KJ heard my cattle joke. And thank God, she thinks I'm funny.

Coming Soon:

Anchored, Book 1 in the Surrendering Opinions Series. Contemporary Romance.

"The Collins Six" made history with their unique birth story, and stayed in the national spotlight with their tragedy.

Now that they are young adults, each sibling tries to find their own identity and romance that matches the love their parents had. Can they surrender the plans and thoughts everyone who helped raise them has and find freedom?

Anchored Prologue

1992

Julia Turmeric stared at the cordless phone in her hand. The buzz of the newsroom swarmed around her, but her focus remained on the disconnected call.

A set of finger snaps brought her back to reality. "Jules! What's going on? I've been talking to you about Hussein's latest statement and I didn't even get an eye roll."

She turned her head to her cameraman and held up the phone. "It's my best friend from back home, Lisa Collins."

Her colleague nodded. "Oh, right. The morning anchor at that little station Upstate, right?"

Julia bit her lip as she replaced the phone to the base. "Yeah. She's pregnant."

"I remember you saying something about it, that her and the husband had been trying for a while. She okay?"

Her expression still vacant, she sighed. "They just learned they are carrying sextuplets. I knew they were doing infertility treatments and there was a chance of multiples, but this?" She ran a finger through her long, ebony, straight hair. "The doctors asked them to reduce, she had some term for it, but she's real serious about her faith. Very pro-life."

He picked up a tripod. "She's keeping all of them?"

She tapped the camera. "And Lisa wants us to document their story."

December, 1992

Julia unbuckled the seatbelt and stared at the ranch-style home in front of her. "How are Lisa and Paul taking care of six babies in this little house?"

Her cameraman took the keys out of the ignition and shrugged. "This is your old Big Flats neighborhood, right? You grew up with brothers and sisters."

She pulled down the visor mirror and applied fresh lipstick. "Not six born at once." She snapped the visor back in place and blotted her mouth with a tissue. "If anyone can do this, it's Lisa. That girl could make the hardest person smile and tell their story to her for the camera. I still don't understand how she didn't keep our pact. In college we said we'd go national together."

"Love will do it all the time." He chuckled. "Ask my ex-wives."

Julia rolled her eyes and gestured toward the house. "Can you get some exterior shots? I'm going in."

She closed her eyes for a moment, and took a deep breath before ringing the doorbell. Julia recognized Lisa's mom, Gail Bell, when she opened the door, cradling a baby.

The instant grandmother of six wore a wide smile. "If it isn't little JT from down the street. Come in."

Julia remembered the childhood name for Lisa's mom. "Hi, Mama G. Who do you have here?"

Gail's shaky laugh echoed in the foyer. "If he didn't have a tag, I wouldn't know. This is James Matthew Collins, number four of six."

Six babies seemed so surreal. Julia looked down the hall and could see a swing in motion.

"My cameraman will be inside soon. We have a lot to do. Can I see Paul and Lisa?"

Mama G. nodded and strolled down the hall to what Julia guessed was a living room. The couch and TV were there, but everything else was baby related. Swings. Baby chairs. Cradles.

Julia could barely take it all in. Two people were in front of her on the couch, each holding a baby. On the floor a woman sat near the swings, watching the remaining three fight sleep as they rocked back and forth.

Gail lowered her voice. "Lisa, Paul. Julian's here."

The two rose from the couch and faced Julia. Lisa navigated through the maze of equipment to reach her friend. "Julia! Thank you so much for doing this. It means everything to Paul and me that you're the one covering our journey."

Julia leaned in for a quick hug. "Are you kidding? Do you know how many stations around the world want to interview the parents of the multiples who not only refused selective reduction, but had them stay the longest in the womb? You all are medical miracles."

Lisa glanced at Paul, who was at her side. "It's all God. He blessed and took care of us."

Paul chuckled. "And we pray He keeps providing. We need all the help we can get."

July 1995

Julia touched the ends of her newly-cut hair. The humidity in New York City seemed extra miserable, but the five-hour trek to Corning didn't seem to provide any relief.

The short hair took getting used to, but she was glad she did it.

Walt shook his head as the Collins home came into view. "Look at all the tricycles."

"It's crazy. At least that means the kids are more mobile than the first time we met them. I can't believe the community pitched in and had this home built for them."

He nodded and pulled into the long, blacktop driveway. Three of the kids were in the yard blowing bubbles. "Viewers eat this up. They love this family. Lisa was smart to lock you in as a lifetime interviewer no matter what job you have, or what station."

Julie smiled. Lisa may have left the news business for home life with the kids, but she was savvy. Every year the media sent Paul and Lisa publicity requests to see the kids and interview them. Lisa found a lawyer willing to draft an exclusive agreement that gave Julia the only access to what reporters called the kids, "The Collins Six."

"And now that I'm co-anchor if Rise and Shine, I think ratings will skyrocket. Moms watch the show, and they adore Lisa." Julia reached for her briefcase and looked out the window. "Speaking of, here she is."

Lisa sauntered over to the news van, her long hair piled on top of her head. "Julia. Walt. It can't be another year already."

The two exited the vehicle and greeted the Faces and Places magazine's Mom of the Year with a hug. "What's three years old like? Does it get worse than terrible two?" Walt opened the back of the van. Lisa shook her head. "All I can say is if your producer wants a transparent look at 'The Collins Six,' you're going to have plenty of footage."

Julia heard a screech, followed by a cry. One of the boys held an empty bubble bottle while one of the girls had wet, soapy hair. Julia tapped her favorite cameraman. "You can start by taping that."

September 1997

Julia tripped over a backpack on her way to the spacious Collins kitchen. Jimmy and Kelly, babies four and five, were eating at the kitchen table. "Hey, guys. Can I ask you a couple questions?"

Jimmy looked to his sister, then to Julia. "Is it for TV?"

She nodded.

He narrowed his eyes and took another bite. "Are you gonna ask about school?"

Julia smiled. "Yes, that's what everyone wants to know about."

He put the bread on the plate. "I can make it easy. We all hate it."

Julia bit her lip to kill the temptation to laugh. She glanced at Kelly, who nodded. "Hate it."

January 2001

Julia placed a piece of hair behind her ear as she looked at her notes for her upcoming interview with the latest A-lister actress. The morning show and evening magazine duties gave her a lot of assignments with Hollywood's elite, but few gave Julia joy in prepping for the meeting.

She took a sip of her coffee and heard a knock on the door. Glancing at her office clock, it was late in the evening for visitors. "Who is it?"

His voice cracked. "Walt."

Julia stood and jogged to the door. He was always home and with his family once his assignments were done. She opened it, ready to invite him in, when she saw his hands shake and his eyes full of tears. "What's wrong?"

"I told the brass I would be the one to tell you."

Her eyebrows furrowed as she tried to discern what he was saying.

"Julia, there's been a terrible accident back in your hometown."

She felt the pit form and enlarge, as she instantly thought of her parents and siblings. "Dad? Mom?"

Walt shook his head. "Lisa and a couple of the kids."

Julia felt her knees sliding beneath her. "Tell me they are okay."

She never, in all her years choosing Walt as her cameraman, saw him cry.

"Lisa's gone."

Acknowledgements:

Hannah: Mrs. Vrabel, thank you for encouraging me and believing in me. For asking about this book and how I am doing.

For the women who have taken time with me, past and present, especially Ms. Lizz, Olivia, Angelina and Mrs. Summer, for spending time with me at Starbucks and getting mani/pedis. For Mr. Duane and Mrs. Tracie and everyone involved in respite nights and Night to Shine for making me feel extra beautiful.

Pastor Matt, Ms. Lizz, Miss Deb, Miss Heidi, Miss Shannon, Miss Susie, Mr. Jason, Mr. Dan and Mrs. Amy, I appreciate you having my back at youth group.

Amilia, Kayla, and Bella, your friendship and encouragement mean so much to me. I love you guys.

For Mrs. Rhonda, for helping us come up with the name of the series just by being Southern.

Cole, Heidi, and your fun families. Thank you for running for me! #coleRuns4Hannah

Randy, Mandy, Oliver, Matt, Stephanie, and James, I love my Wisconsin family.

Grandma, Aunt Crista, and Landon. You always cheer me on. Thank you!

Brian, you're a great brother, even if I pretend to be annoyed by you.

Dad, thanks for everything you do for our family and how you make me smile. And for lunch money.

Mom, thanks for taking me out of my comfort zone by hearing my story idea and making it real. For believing in me.

Jesus, You told my parents before I was born that I would be an overcomer. Thank You for being a keeper of promises.

Julie: Hannah, you challenge and inspire me daily to keep shining bright for Christ even when times are tough. In a difficult season, you chose better over bitter. More than that, you came up with a series that I believe was God sent to encourage many. You are amazing.

Scribes 202, this book wasn't a normal submission given my contemporary romance background, but you dove in without reservation or hesitation. Thank you for all your help. I couldn't write without you.

The Johnson family. Thank you for inspiring Jazmin and everything we love about her.

Alanis Royce, we so appreciate the time you gave us looking over and fixing the dance aspects of the manuscript.

Shirley, Ruth, Kara, Deb, Tracie, Summer, Brenda, Rita, Noreen, and Amy. Your prayers literally cover everything in my life. Thank you for keeping this project and our family in prayer.

Pastor Gary and Rhonda Gray for allowing me to share sermon notes, and for Rhonda inspiring the name of the series and being all around wonderful.

Randy, Mandy, Oliver, Matt, Stephanie, and James, thank you for loving Hannah, Brian, and me from the first moment we entered your lives.

Brian, you had your own refiner's fire at the same time Hannah was trusting God through hers. The pure gold that is showing itself from that season blesses and teaches me. Keep believing Him, even and especially when the world disappoints.

Tom, thanks for being among the first to show me true freedom comes when I surrender negative thinking. I've grown because you taught me to give people the benefit of the doubt, and reminded me that God promised to lead us through the fire, not around it. Thanks for asking.

Jesus, I didn't see any of this coming, the adversity or the story. You did, and I appreciate the grace as I processed the hurt, grief, lament, and the beginning of healing. Not a word, not a breath is possible without You. It is all for the furthering of Your Kingdom and Your glory.

Other Julie Arduini Titles

Surrendering Time Series

(Contemporary Romance)

Entrusted:

A city-girl produces a lot of change for a mountain grocer. A romance about surrendering loss, change, and wanting to belong. This is a free eBook on juliearduini.com.

Entangled:

A single mom has been given everything to make her dreams come true, but regret keeps her from enjoying her blessings. Can her reliable, truck-driving boyfriend help her surrender her past?

Engaged:

A career woman returns to her rural hometown after her dreams crumble and she has no other plans. Can the local paramedic come to her rescue?

Finding Freedom Through Surrender: A 30-Day Devotional:

Features the characters and themes from Entrusted, Entangled, and Engaged. Perfect whether you've enjoyed or are new to the series.

Multi-Author Devotional
Workbook about Infertility

A Walk in the Valley: Six authors share their own infertility stories from diagnosis to where they are now. Includes questions for reflection.

The Julie Arduini Newsletter

Subscribe and receive free eBook of Entrusted, Book 1 in the Surrendering Time Series. Monthly-or-so email with writing updates, recipes, giveaways, contests, book recommendations and more. Visit juliearduini.com to subscribe for free.

Fall in Love with a Good Book

Follow Julie Arduini and other Inspy Romance authors:

Blog:

http://inspyromance.com

Twitter:

http://twitter.com/inspyromance

Facebook:

http://facebook.com/inspyromance

Pinterest:

http://pinterest.com/inspyromance

CHRISTIANS READ

Follow Julie Arduini and other Christian authors at Christians Read.

Blog:

http://christiansread.wordpress.com

Facebook:

http://facebook.com/christiansread

Twitter:

http://twitter.com/christiansread

Looking for

an Encouraging Speaker?

Julie Arduini is passionate about encouraging audiences to find freedom through surrender. She's able to speak on a wide range of surrender topics, the writing process, family, motherhood, and her own books.

Learn more by contacting her at juliearduini@juliearduini.com.

Regan's Acts of Kindness

Although I never met Regan, her parents spent a lot of time with our family when we lived in Upstate NY. Regan was taken from them in January 2017. She would have turned five in March.

Everyone who loved Regan wants her to be remembered.

Here are different ways you can help make that happen:

Like Regan's Acts of Kindness on Facebook and participate.
http://facebook.com/RegansActsofKindness

Paint Rocks and Hide Them in Appropriate Places in Your Community. Check the Facebook page above to learn how to tag them to keep the kindness flowing.

Visit Regan's Corner at The Wild Animal Park in Chittenango, New York http://thewildpark.com

About the Authors:

Hannah Arduini is in the ninth grade and lives outside of Youngstown, Ohio. She loves fashion, Starbucks, and serving at church. She has a brother who lives at home, and siblings that live in Wisconsin. She also has two nephews. *You're Amazing* is her second published book.

Julie Arduini loves to encourage readers to find freedom in Christ by surrendering the good, the bad, and---maybe one day---the chocolate. She's the author of the contemporary romance series Surrendering Time, featuring ENTRUSTED, ENTANGLED, and ENGAGED. FINDING FREEDOM THROUGH SURRENDER is her 30-day devotional using the surrender themes and characters from the series. She shares her infertility story in A WALK IN THE VALLEY. RESTORING CHRISTMAS, a Christian romance, will re-release in November 2019.

She blogs every other Wednesday for Christians Read, and also is a blogger for Inspy Romance. She resides in Ohio with her husband and two children. Learn more by visiting her at http://juliearduini.com.